I0763514

THE PHANTOM TRAIN

The Phantom Train

ISBN: (hardback)
(paperback)
(ebook)

Printed in the United States of America

THE PHANTOM TRAIN

A Jeannie Loomis Novel

GARY J. ROSE

For Mike and Mary Lake

for reading my early drafts and assisting

in the plot and subplots

of this novel.

What readers are saying about
The Fourth Reich and Black Heart/Black Cell:

The Fourth Reich

5.0 out of 5 stars

An Exiting Story That Checks All the Right Boxes

Reviewed in the United States on March 22, 2022

I've always enjoyed historical fiction, especially books centered around the events of World War II. This highly entertaining novel is a mixture of Science-Fiction, Alternate History, Suspense, Thriller, and Mystery. While a work of fiction, there are many interesting and historically accurate facts contained in the book. The prologue at the beginning of the book was a nice added touch to bring readers up to speed on relevant facts about Nazi Germany and cloning. It nicely set the stage for the rest of the book. The story is fast-paced, full of unexpected twists and a great plot. The characters are interesting, and I especially enjoyed FBI Special Agent Jeannie Loomis.

5.0 out of 5 stars

Interesting

Reviewed in the United States on March 16, 2022

This was an interesting read with an amazing plot. I find cloning an interesting subject and the thought of Hitler really being cloned is terrifying. It could very well happen in our lifetimes which makes this all the scarier. The characters were fleshed out and compelling and made me care about them. The twists and turns kept me reading until the end. I recommend this book if you want a page-turner and compelling read.

5.0 out of 5 stars

I'm in love

Reviewed in the United States on November 24, 2021

I didn't know when I picked up this book that there were more out there, but now I'm excited to read the rest. However, this one is perfect as a standalone, so it didn't distract me any. The concept of cloning Hitler was beyond interesting for me, as I've always been in love with World War 2 History, and the characters, concepts, twists, and turns kept me on the edge of my seat and turning pages to see what happens next. I was sucker punched throughout this entire book, and I loved every moment of it. Thank you so much for a thrilling ride! I can't wait to read the rest in the series.

5.0 out of 5 stars

Great blend of history, drama, and romance

Reviewed in the United States on May 12, 2022

This was my first reading of a book within the series of novels featuring FBI agent Jeannie Loomis. At the start, there was a relatively brief but detailed outline concerning the science of cloning and the historical connection to Nazi Germany. This helped with setting the stage for the main plot. Once the story begins, it moves quickly. The good people and bad people are obvious. No guesswork involved. But the development of the plot kept me turning pages. There are some typical buddy-cop interactions and of course ruthless Nazis-type activity. Yet, there is also a touch of romance spiced with humor. The ending brought sufficient resolution to the story while leaving me wondering how the unresolved subplots will be addressed in the next book. I will read the next book!

5.0 out of 5 stars

Darkly suspenseful

Reviewed in the United States on April 24, 2022

Verified Purchase

This book's jarring content is well woven into a frighteningly well-conceived plot that cleverly brings the wickedness of the Third Reich into a new chapter where the terror of a Fourth is dawning as wheels turn and experiments push forward a new Nazi power. It is well written, fast-paced and an all and all entertaining read. I would, however, advise caution as its content may not be for sensitive readers, or especially those who experienced the horrors of the concentration camps of WW2 first hand.

5.0 out of 5 stars

Intense

Reviewed in the United States on June 16, 2022

Well-researched and written, this dark story paints a vivid picture of madness. Warning this book isn't for anyone faint of heart. It's an intense thriller, borderline horror novel filled with mystery, suspense, and fear.

Black Heart/Black Cell

5.0 out of 5 stars

Intense

Reviewed in the United States on August 11, 2022

Thrilling, twisting FBI plots, starting with the blackout of the Super Bowl by a group of international hackers, and an additional plot of a serial killer who kidnaps his female prey only to hunt them down later. FBI Agent Jeannie Loomis kicks butt.

4.0 out of 5 stars

Witty and filled with action and adventure

Reviewed in the United States on August 3, 2022

This action and adventure story has a strong female protagonist, FBI Agent Jeannie Loomis who has become my female superhero. She has so great things to say in this book while facing suspension and aid the Idaho State Police, investigation a serial killer in the wilderness. While this is the eighth book in the series, it is easy to read on its own without getting lost or feeling like you are missing something. Good writing. Great editing. This was a very enjoyable read.

5.0 de 5 estrellas

Fast paced must read!

Calificado en Estados Unidos el 1 de agosto de 2022

Multiple intertwining plots in this thriller novel. As the main character, kickass FBI Agent Jeannie Loomis, investigates a serial killer case while on suspension, her boyfriend, Interpol Agent Sean Delaney, investigation a Super Bowl hack by a gang who fancies itself as modern day Robin Hoods. She also resolves a personal case of becoming the unexpected sole heir to an aunt's estate. Hats of to the writer for masterfully weaving the three storylines, yet having the novel be a stand-alone. I strongly recommend this fast-paced page turner! Can't wait to read this author's other books.

Other Jeannie Loomis novels:

Ark of the Covenant – Raid on the Church of Our Lady Mary of Zion

Star Chamber

Forgotten Plans

House of Special Purpose

Time Game

Thin Blue Line

The Fourth Reich

Black Heart/Black Cell

Prologue

Nazi plunder (Raubkunst) was the organized looting of European countries during the time of the Nazi Party in Germany. It began in 1933, first with the seizure of property from German Jews but then extended into all the occupied territories of Nazi Germany until the end of World War II. Paintings, sculptures, gold, silver, jewelry, books, and religious treasures were stolen along with items from Jews deported to concentration and death camps.

Between 1933 and 1945, Nazi Germany and its allies established more than 44,000 camps and other incarceration sites, including ghettos. The perpetrators used these sites for a range of purposes, including forced labor, detention of people thought to be enemies of the state, and mass murder, especially of Jews.

Killing centers were designed and built to carry out genocide. Between 1941 and 1945, the Nazis established six killing centers in eastern Poland, Chelmno, Belzec, Sobibor, Treblinka, Auschwitz-Birkenau, and Majdanek. An estimated 3.5 million Jews were killed in these six camps alone.

After training, SS officers commanded all the concentration camps in Germany and German-occupied territory while units known as SS Death head units (*SS-Totenkopfverbande*) guarded and administered the camps. The daily life of prisoners lay in the brutal and merciless hands of the camp commandants and these SS Death head units.

There, the victims had to strip completely before being murdered, and all their personal belongings were confiscated. These valuable items included gold, coins, rings, spectacles, jewelry, and other precious metals. After their gassing, it also included the removal of any gold and silver teeth fillings, which were eventually converted to bullion.

An example of how this was instituted is after Nazi Germany's annexation of Austria; on April 26, 1938, the "Decree for the Reporting of Jewish-Owned Property" was issued by Hitler's government, which, when it took effect, required all Jews in both Germany and Austria to register any property or assets valued at more than 5,000 *Reichsmarks* (around $2,000 in American currency of the period, or $34,000 today).

From furniture and paintings to life insurance and stocks, nothing was immune from the registry. By July 31 of that year, German finance officials had collected paperwork from some 700,000 Jewish citizens with seven billion *Reichsmarks*-worth of wealth ripe for state-sanctioned theft known as "Aryanization."

Hitler planned to use the wealth generated from this looting to establish the European Art Museum in Linz, Austria. In "his" museum, he would display his new personal collection of seized art by the Old Masters, particularly those of Germanic origin. Due to the large amount of treasure being accumulated, high-ranking officials like Hermann Goering also added to their personal collections.

Hitler later assigned Goering to oversee and supervise the seizure and storage of the Nazis' stolen wealth. In 1940, Goering commanded that the loot would first be divided between Hitler and himself. Hitler later ordered that all confiscated works of art were to be made directly available to him. Items that Hitler and Goering did not want were made available to other Nazi leaders.

The Third Reich amassed hundreds of thousands of objects from occupied nations and stored them in several key locations, including the Musee Jeu de Paume in Paris and the Nazi headquarters in Munich. Some were stored at Hitler's final residence, his Führer bunker in Berlin.

As allied forces gained the advantage in the war and began bombing German cities and historic institutions, Germany began storing these artworks in salt mines and caves for protection. These mines and caves offered appropriate humidity and temperature conditions for delicate artworks. The mines were not only used for the storage of looted art but also for gold, silver, and jewelry.

The total cost of German Nazi theft and destruction of Polish art alone is estimated at fifty billion dollars in today's dollars.

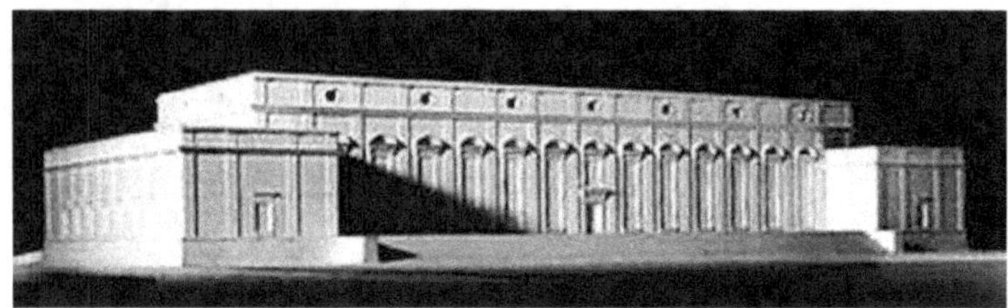

Unrealized Führermuseaum, also called the Linz art gallery, was the destination for much of the stolen Nazi loot. Hitler wanted to fill his Führermuseaum with the greatest art treasures in the world and believed that most of the world's finest art belonged to Germany after having been looted during the Napoleonic and First World Wars.

As World War II was drawing toward a close, the Nazis constructed a series of underground tunnels. There are many theories about the real purpose of those tunnels. One is that they were to become Hitler's many bunkers. Other theories have the tunnels being a place for secret arms manufacturing on the lines of the V-2 rocket. Still others believe they were constructed as safe places for the remaining Nazi hierarchy to wait out the war.

Rumors also persisted that Martin Bormann, Hitler's private secretary, was the brainchild of a further plan to smuggle the Nazi hierarchy and the treasures stolen by Nazi aggression to South America on U-boats, specifically Argentina. He tried, unsuccessfully, to convince Hitler to flee via a U-Boat, but instead, he tried to turn the outcome of the war around while in his bunker, culminating in his suicide.

Records show that twelve U-boats were used in the transportation of these items, but at the end of the war, all twelve were accounted for, and no trace of their purported treasures has been found.

Most treasure hunters, and even some highly regarded historians, believe that the plan under Goering is much more believable. The rumor was that a gold-laden train, a phantom train, was hidden in a cavernous abode. In fact, not just one train, but many. Regardless of which rumor is correct, if any are, one undeniable fact is that many human lives were lost during their construction.

Hermann Goering

After Hitler's appointment as Chancellor of Germany in 1933, Goering took on many positions of power and leadership within the Nazi state, including the commander in chief of the *Luftwaffe* (German air force), director of the four-year plan for the German economy, and, at the outbreak of war in Europe, Hitler's acknowledged successor. It was Goering who commanded Secret Police Chief Reinhard Heydrich to organize and coordinate the "final solution" to the Jewish question.

Sobibor Death Camp – March 25, 1943

In 1942, Heinrich Himmler's Operation Reinhard, part of the final solution to the Jewish question, authorized the construction of three secret death camps in eastern Poland. Those camps were Belzec, Treblinka, and the most secret, Sobibor.

Sobibor was an extermination camp established and operated by the SS solely as a killing center devoted exclusively to or primarily for the elimination of Jews in gas chambers. From April 1942 to mid-October 1943, the German SS and their auxiliaries, mainly Ukrainian guards, killed at least 167,000 people.

The camp was built along the Lublin-Chelm-Wlodawa railway line just west of Sobibor railway station. A nearby spur connected the railway to the camp and was used to offload prisoners from incoming transports. A dense forest of pine and birch shielded the site from view.

"I just received word that in two days, Reichsmarschall Goering will be visiting Sobibor and presenting you with an award for your expansion of the railroad line into the camp," SS-Obergruppenführer Oswald Pohl stated. He stood six feet tall and was large all over, weighing over 225 pounds. With striking blue eyes and jet-black hair, he was a poster boy for the Aryan race, especially for the SS. He also wore glasses similar in style to those worn by Henrich Himmler, which Detwrick thought was the only reason he wore them since he knew they were not prescription glasses.

"I admit it was a brilliant idea and greatly reduced the number of Jews attempting to escape when their transport trains arrived. I am informed that it will be a short ceremony since the Reichsmarschall must return to Berlin."

"Thank you. I look forward to meeting the Reichsmarschall," said a stunned Lieutenant Franz Detwrick, still standing at attention. Detwrick was only five feet ten inches tall and thinly built, but his blond hair and blue eyes would have met with approval from Henrich Himmler as an example of the supreme race. He took pride in his highly polished jackboots and SS uniform, preferring the black version.

"That will be in two days. Tomorrow morning, I want the Sonderkommandos for crematorium two to be changed and the selection of their replacements completed without delay. Do I make myself clear?" Obergruppenführer Oswald Pohl asked.

The Sonderkommandos were groups of Jewish prisoners forced to perform a variety of duties in the gas chambers and crematoria of the Nazi camp system. They worked primarily in the Nazi killing centers, like Auschwitz, but they were also used at other killing sites to dispose of the victims' corpses.

The Sonderkommandos were granted much less squalid living conditions than the other inmates because the Germans needed them to remain physically able. They slept in their own barracks and were allowed to keep and use various goods like food, medicines, and cigarettes brought into the camp by those who were sent to the gas chambers.

Unlike ordinary inmates, they were not normally subject to arbitrary killing by guards. How they lived and for how long were determined by how efficiently they could keep the Nazi death factory running. As a result, Sonderkommando members survived longer in the death camps than other prisoners, but few survived the war.

Since they had detailed knowledge of the Nazis' practice of mass murder, the Sonderkommando were bearers of secrets. As such, they were held in isolation away from prisoners being used as slave labor. Every three months, according to SS policy, almost all the Sonderkommandos working in the death camps' killing areas would be gassed and replaced with new arrivals to ensure secrecy. However, some inmates survived for up to a year or more because they possessed specialist skills.

"Jawohl, Herr Obergruppenführer," Lt. Detwrick shouted while snapping his boots together and giving the Hitler salute. He then turned and left the Obergruppenführer's office and began walking towards crematorium two. He never got used to the smell of the black smoke billowing from the large smokestack. He watched for a moment as the smoke rose. *They smell just as bad as when they were alive*, he told himself. *The Reichsmarschall is coming here to see me.*

Before reaching the crematorium, he crossed near a long line of female Jews and children preparing to enter the changing room and watched the whole process begin. A Jewish orchestra played some tune the name of which he could not recall, hoping to lull the Jews into entering the changing room without rebelling. Some children cried while mothers held their hands or held them, depending on their ages.

Once they entered the changing room, a Sonderkommando instructed them to take off their shoes, tie them together, and place them with their clothing under a numbered hook on the wall so they could find them easily when they returned from their hot shower. He knew they would not be reclaiming them, but if he shared that information, he would be shot on the spot.

The women were directed to a shearing room where, under the pretense of stopping an infection of lice, they had their hair cut off. Any children with long hair endured the same treatment. The Jews were then told to fall in line and follow the person in front of them to the showers as they tried to cover their bodies while taking care of their children. The floors were wet, and the walls were clean and white. Brand new shower heads hung from the ceiling. "Naturally, there would be water on the floor; it was the shower room," thought many as they entered the large room. They did not notice the absence of water droplets coming from the sprinkler heads.

After the room was packed with victims, sometimes up to 450 at a time, the door was sealed, and the lights quickly turned off, throwing the shower room into complete darkness and panic. Children and babies screamed as they clung even tighter to their mothers. A heavy diesel engine installed on a cement base outside the shower room had pipes leading from their exhaust manifold into the gas chamber to provide the carbon monoxide gas when turned on.

The smell of gas spewing from the shower heads began consuming the remaining air. People began gagging, and several began urinating and defecating on the floor. More and more bodies began falling to the floor, only to have others climb on top of them to get to the last remnants of oxygen. Within twenty to thirty minutes, all those inside were dead.

The whole process, from arrival to cremation, took only two or three hours. During that time, other prisoners were forced to clean the railroad cars, after which the trains left, and another twenty cars entered the camp.

The SS guard opened his small viewing window and looked into the shower room for any movement. Seeing none, he turned on the ventilation fans, allowing the gas to be expelled. A few minutes later, the Sonderkommandos were allowed to enter.

Their first job was to pull the bodies apart since there was a huge pile in the center of the room where the stronger people had stood on the bodies of the weaker to get to the remaining oxygen. It was hard work since the urine and fecal matter made the floors slippery. As the bodies were pulled apart, the victim's mouth was forced open, and any teeth with gold or silver fillings were quickly pulled out with the use of pliers.

The gold and silver-filled teeth were placed in a pocket and would later be turned over to the SS. The victim's vagina and anal cavity were also explored, and any hidden jewelry was confiscated. As each body was examined for gold fillings and other valuables, another Sonderkommando unit would drag the body from the shower room and place it on a cart destined for the crematorium.

After the task was complete and the room cleared of bodies, a final team of Sonderkommandos quickly rinsed down the floor and washed the walls, preparing for the next arrivals.

Periodically, the crematorium ovens were cooled, allowing for the accumulation of ash to be scraped out, placed in wheelbarrows, and finally deposited in dump trucks that would deliver the ash to local farmers to be used as fertilizer. The Nazis made sure not one part of a Jew went to waste.

After only a few months of operation, the wooden walls of the gas chambers had absorbed too much sweat, urine, blood, and excrement to be cleanable. Thus, the gas chambers were demolished in the summer of 1942, and new, larger ones were built out of brick. Later that summer, the SS also embarked on a beautification project, instituting a more regular cleaning schedule for the barracks, and expanding and landscaping the *Vorlager* to give it the appearance of a "Tyrolean village."

Detwrick's job was to oversee the Sonderkommandos at all stages of the process.

The shiny black Mercedes Benz 770 arrived at the front gate at 8:15 in the morning. Two trucks carrying SS personnel preceded the vehicle. The SS staff and the Ukrainian guards at Sobibor jockeyed for the best viewing positions to see the second most powerful person in Nazi Germany, Reichsmarschall Hermann Goering.

The commandant stood in front of his office, waiting for the reichsmarschall's car and entourage to stop. Before Goering exited his vehicle, a contingent of SS guards surrounded it. Although no attempts had been made on his life, that could not be said about Adolf Hitler. Finally, with the protective guards in place, the driver opened a rear door of the Mercedes and out stepped Goering wearing his favorite powder blue uniform and carrying a jewel-encrusted baton.

Detwrick was aware that Goering had taken part in the abortive Beer Hall Putsch in November 1923, in which Hitler tried to seize power prematurely. During the putsch, Goering was badly wounded in the groin. His arrest was ordered, but he escaped into Austria with his wife. He was given morphine to deaden the pain from his wounds and became so severely addicted that he twice underwent treatment in a mental hospital in Sweden in 1925 and 1926.

In 1927, he returned to Germany, where his contacts in German industry proved useful, and he was taken back into the party leadership. He occupied one of the twelve Reichstag seats that the Nazi Party won in the 1928 election. Thereafter, Goering became the acknowledged party leader in the lower house, and when the Nazis won 230 seats in the election of July 1932, he was elected president of the Reichstag. Goering's position as Hitler's most loyal supporter remained unassailable for the rest of the decade.

Detwrick knew that the morphine addiction added to Goering's egocentric and bombastic personality and his delight in dressing in flamboyant clothes and uniforms, decorations, and exhibitionist jewelry. He really made quite a sight when you saw him in person.

He was greeted by SS-Obergruppenführer Oswald Pohl. Lieutenant Detwrick stood next to Pohl. After pleasantries were exchanged, Goering looked at his driver, who handed him a blue velvet box which, everyone knew, contained the medal that Detwrick would be awarded for his work in Sobibor.

After a speech that was short by Goering's standard, he opened the small box, removed the medal, and pinned it on the Detwrick's uniform. "And now, Obergruppenführer, I would like the use of your office for a few minutes so I can discuss something with the lieutenant."

1

CHAPTER

JEANNIE WOKE TO her cell phone vibrating on the nightstand. "Hey, you still in bed? About time you earned your huge salary. I can't keep covering your ass." Grabbing her alarm clock, she realized it was almost 9:15. She had overslept. She should have been at her desk in San Francisco by now. The FBI Assistant Special Agent in Charge could not believe that she had somehow slept right through her alarm, or did she forget to set it?

"Good morning, Ace," she said as she sat up in bed, scratching her scalp through her long blond hair. "And I bet you just love catching me in bed at this hour." Her partner, colleague, and best friend, Agent Ismail Flores, loved to rib her any chance he got, and boy did he get her today. Jeannie was not the type to ignore an alarm and being late for anything was unacceptable.

She turned her alarm clock around and noticed that she had forgotten to set the alarm. *Getting old, girl.* "Shit, I overslept. Tell Lomax I am sorry, but I will get my ass there ASAP. And as for you, make sure your stuff is out of my office, including your 8x10 self-portrait and all the food wrappers you have stuffed in my desk drawers."

"Gee, I cover for you all these weeks, and that's the gratitude I get," he replied while laughing. "Be safe on the ride in, and I will put the coffee on. Lot of wackos on the road, you know."

Ismail was more like a brother than a fellow agent. Together, he and the rest of her team had solved some very big cases for the San Francisco bureau. Over the years, they had taken down the mysterious Star Chamber court and several of their assassins but initially failed to bring down their ringleader, Joey. They later caught up with him and the remnants of his group of urban terrorists, only to get engaged in a massive firefight that resulted in the death of her fiancé and Ismail's cousin, NSA agent Ricky Pinheiro.

There was also the investigation of jihadists who were planning to blow up the underwater tube of the Bay Area rapid transit system than ran between Oakland and San Francisco. This was initiated on orders from Osama bin Laden to be carried out upon his death.

Recently, they broke up a group of modern-day Nazis who were intent on creating a Fourth Reich through cloning. Not just any cloning, however, but the cloning of Adolf Hitler himself through DNA they had stolen from the Russians.

Ismail was a twenty-five-year veteran of the FBI. A shade under six feet and in great shape, which he would remind anyone who would listen, he gave up on combing over what hair remained and now only had hair on the sides of his head. His mustache was always immaculately trimmed, and he never seemed to put on weight even though he always complained of being hungry.

They had been partners for more years than Jeannie could count. He stayed at her side in the hospital after she was shot by an urban terrorist group, losing her unborn child in the process. She wasn't sure who the father was since her pregnancy resulted from one of many alcoholic blackouts, but since that time, she had been trying to clean up her act.

His family was her family. With two failed marriages under her belt and the recent death of Ricky, she relied on their love more than ever. Birthdays and major holidays were normally spent together, and his wife was like a sister.

Yes, she and Ismail could write a weekly TV series about their cases, but mainstream television wasn't interested in that type of programming anymore, it seemed. As her mom and dad used to say, "Gone are the days of Father Knows Best, Gunsmoke, Bonanza, Ozzie and Harriet, and even Walt Disney. To Jeannie, society seemed to have gone upside down, and she did not base that solely on the scum she dealt with daily.

For years, she and Ismail had been able to fly under the radar politically, even escaping involvement directly or indirectly in the corruption at the top of the bureau. A lot of that credit, however, was due to their outstanding boss, their SAC (Special Agent in Charge), Lomax.

Lomax was pushing almost thirty years with the FBI and appeared to be unscathed by the bullshit in D.C. He just seemed to have the knack of avoiding involvement in political infighting among the brass above him, which included protecting his team of agents in San Francisco. Being the head honcho in the liberal city and still being respected by both the left and the right as a no-nonsense administrator said a lot about his leadership abilities.

It was Friday morning, and she had decided, with the approval of her supervisor, SAC Lomax, to return to work for one day and then start the next week off fresh. She had just returned from an east coast visit while on paid suspension, telling everyone that she had always wanted to take a cross-country trip. The real reason was to investigate her birth mother, who wasn't the woman who had raised her. She had kept this recently learned information to herself. With that new knowledge, she also learned that, through her inheritance, she was an extremely wealthy woman. "Extremely" being the operative word.

She jumped into a hot shower and shampooed her hair. She would let it dry during the drive into the city. Once she got there, she would put it in a ponytail. She glanced at herself in her full-length mirror while toweling herself off. *Not bad for a 40-something female.* She put on her Victoria's Secret panties and bra (*a girl must be prepared)* and black slacks topped off with a long-sleeved blue blouse. *You dressed in layers in the City by the Bay.*

Blond-haired with blue eyes, she stood 5'6", 130 pounds, and was muscular enough to make most men think twice about talking back to her. She looked like the kind of woman who wouldn't be out of place leading a Viking raiding party, and she could still turn heads when she entered a room.

While getting dressed and thinking of her physical appearance, she remembered her fiancé comparing her to Laura Vandervoort, a Canadian actress who, at the time, was thirty-seven years old. Jeannie last saw her in a 2021 movie called Trigger Point, where she played a detective in a murder case. Jeannie liked the comparison.

Downstairs she found three pieces of French toast in her freezer that she quickly popped into the toaster while pouring a cup of left-over coffee. She placed the coffee in her microwave and pulled out the French toast from the toaster. While the coffee was heating up, she grabbed some syrup from the refrigerator. A paper towel placed on her kitchen counter became her plate on which she poured some syrup. She dunked a strip of French toast into the syrup and chewed it while removing the coffee. "Who says I can't multi-task?" she said to no one.

A stop at her aquarium in the dining room to feed her koi and tell them what she had planned for the day, and she was off to the garage after grabbing her purse and firearm. *God, I hope I don't run into Delores,* she thought as she jumped into her Vette while opening the garage door with her fob. At the last minute, there Delores stood, blocking the driveway and making Jeannie feel irritated.

"Hi, Delores, I'm really sorry, but a big case just broke, and I need to run. Talk to you when I get back." Delores just waved and stepped aside. *No more Delores, yeah. Dumbarton Bridge, here I come.* After thinking about how she just treated Delores, she felt bad since Delores and her husband Walter were great neighbors.

They not only watched her place when she was absent, but they also took care of her koi and garbage can. The two, unknowingly at the time, had even provided solutions to several of her cases.

In some ways, Delores was like the fictional character Grandma Mazur in Janet Evanovich's Stephanie Plum series.

There was never a time when a commute from Newark to the City by the Bay was uncongested. Those days, like quality television, were gone. Too many people, a collapsing infrastructure, high taxes, drought; *hell, what else could a person ask for?* But she was still in a good mood and couldn't wait to see her team.

Perhaps all she had learned from her recent trip to Myrtle Beach, South Carolina, and the discovery that the woman she had known as mom was her aunt and an unknown aunt was her biological mother caused her to forget to set her alarm. Who knows?

She rolled down the passenger window of her Corvette and allowed the wind to dry her hair while still trying to rationalize the events in the last week or so of her life. She had received a phone call from an estate attorney notifying her that she was the only heir to a person she did not know. As she tried to get her head around this bit of information, she discovered that her real mom was an unknown aunt who lived in Myrtle Beach, South Carolina, and was extremely wealthy.

A letter found in her safe deposit box explained everything, but she was still processing it and had not shared it with anyone, including Ismail. Why, she didn't know, but the more she thought about it, the more she felt a need to keep it quiet for the time being.

2

CHAPTER

"MOMMA, DO I have to go?" Anna Hetman asked her mother, who was laying out her best black outfit. A typical seventeen-year-old, Anna would be more content staying home texting her friends or playing a video game. She wore her hair loose, hanging down over her shoulders with bangs in the front. She was fortunate not to have to battle acne at her age but was sad that her boobs were smaller than her girlfriends at school. She told her mom several times that she needed a boob job, but her mother insisted that her body was just fine.

Anna's great uncle's death was not unexpected since he had lived until he was 101 years old. Not a small feat, Anna's mother said, knowing what he had gone through during the war.

Anna's mom used to tell her stories after they visited Uncle Detwrick, but Anna was too busy with social media to care.

"That is what's wrong with your generation," her mother would always say. "You do not study history in school and will not know when it repeats itself for the worse. Yes, young lady, you are going to the funeral. You have eleven minutes to get ready."

She did not try to hide what Uncle Detwrick had done in the war from Anna as others do with dark family secrets. Anna knew that he served his sentence in prison after World War II and later came to the United States with his wife, and they never seemed to have any financial problems.

"But mom, we both know he was a Nazi SS officer. I never really knew him. He was kinda creepy. I wish he had died during the war, especially after what he must have done to the Jews in those camps. He didn't care about me as most uncles would."

"Anna, I am also ashamed about the part your uncle played in the war, but he was convicted of his crimes and served over 30 years for what he did. We can at least pay our last respects."

"Okay, I'll go, but he will not get any respect from me."

There were only nine people in attendance as the priest said what they normally say at a funeral. Detwrick had outlived most of his immediate family members and friends. In the final years of his life, he rarely went outside, relying on his next-door neighbors to bring him groceries and take him to the doctor's office. They made up the few in attendance at his funeral. Secretive was probably the best way to describe his last twenty years. However, his mind had remained sharp until the last year. He loved playing on his computer, researching God knew what.

Nola, his only living relative, rarely had contact with him since she hated seeing his display of SS medals hanging on the wall, including a disgusting picture of Hendrick Himmler and Adolf Hitler. She would only be civil with him, occasionally bringing a store-bought cake on his birthday and leaving it on the table. She never brought him a gift. Come to think of it, after her little discourse with Anna she realized she normally stayed less than ten minutes when she visited him.

Being his only listed heir, she and Anna would start cleaning up his house on Saturday to get it ready for sale. For Anna, the only interesting thing about the house was its proximity to Chinatown with its great Chinese restaurants. Nola enticed her daughter with a $15 an hour salary to get her to agree to spend her weekend in the gloomy house that, she said, smelled old.

Nola Hetman was employed as a full-time federal court interpreter with the Administrative Office of the US Courts. Her most recent case involved the Russian mafia, which was fascinating but, at the same time, exhausting. Only one of the accused spoke

English, so while the court was in session, she was constantly interpreting what was being said. If she and Anna could clean up the house quickly and sell it, she would inherit a considerable sum of money with the real estate market being out of control in the city. With the inheritance, she could retire earlier than planned.

Bright and early, too early according to Anna, they arrived at Detwrick's residence. They did not notice a newer model blue Ford F 150 parked two houses down facing the residence. Nola opened the trunk of her car and pulled out two buckets, some rolls of paper towels, and some cleaning products while handing Anna some rubber gloves, a mop, and a broom. "Let's getter done," Nola said in her best Larry the Cable Guy's voice as Anna rolled her eyes.

Opening the front door, Nola had to admit that Anna was right. The place smelled old. *Oh well, with a good cleaning and a quick paint job by a bargain painting company, it should sell quickly.* Anna was given the three bedrooms while Nola tackled the two bathrooms and kitchen.

After working for about twenty-five minutes, Nola heard a knock on the front door. She took off her gloves, wiped the sweat from her hands and opened it. Two men stood there, one with a gun pointed at her. "Don't scream, or I'll shoot you. Get back inside." Nola reached for her mouth while backing away from the front door. "Where's the little bitch?" one of the men asked. Nola did not say anything but pointed down the hallway to the bedrooms.

"Please, don't hurt her. Take whatever you want."

The second person, also with a gun in his hand, walked down the hallway while Nola was told to sit on a kitchen chair. "What the fuck?" Nola heard her daughter say from a bedroom, followed by what sounded like a hard slap. Soon, Anna walked down the hallway holding her cheek, followed by her escort. She was placed in a chair across from her mom.

"We do not want to hurt you. The quicker you give us the map, the quicker we will leave." Both had heavy German accents while speaking broken English.

"What map? What are you talking about?" Nola said.

"You know what map. The map of the tunnel with the gold train."

"I don't know what you are talking about. You must have the wrong house. This is the house of my uncle who recently died. He was over 100 years old. We are just cleaning up the place so we can sell it."

Before she could react, the barrel of a gun caught her on the bridge of her nose, breaking it and spewing blood across the floor. "Stop it, you asshole! Let my mom alone. She is telling the truth!"

The gunman near Anna pulled some plastic ties from his pocket and cuffed Anna's legs

to the chair and her hands behind her back. He handed some ties to his partner, who did the same to

Nola. Once secured, Anna's blouse was ripped open, showing her red bra. Nola screamed, followed by another slap of the gun on the crown of her head.

Pulling out a knife, the front of Anna's bra was sliced open, freeing her breasts. "Not bad," he said. "Shame if I have to fuck you and then cut them off." He looked at Nola with a sneer on his face.

***

Jeannie spent most of Friday telling everyone who wanted to know about her cross-country trip from what she called Wacko, California to Myrtle Beach, South Carolina, via the southern route. Of course, she had to field questions about alligators, eating grits, and whether she liked sweet tea. Jeannie didn't mind telling the same stories repeatedly. It was just nice to get back into the swing of things while she still wondered what to do with her newfound wealth.

"Sorry you had to move your big screen television and hot tub out of my office," Jeannie said to Ismail when he arrived, clutching a cup of coffee.

"Well, you know, your office is kinda small for someone with my talent and abilities. When I am ready to move up, I will request a much bigger abode."

"Really. And when might that be?" asked SAC Lomax, who had walked up undetected and was standing behind Ismail with a smile on his face. "You know, there is an opening now in Fairbanks, Alaska."

"Oh, hello, boss. I, I was just bringing Loomis up to speed since she's been gone so long. Talk to you later," he said to Jeannie as he quickly made his retreat.

Lomax grinned, looking at Jeannie. "Once again, he did a great job while you were gone. He'll make an excellent supervisor soon, I expect. The troops have a lot of respect for him. I just hope Washington doesn't transfer him somewhere once they recognize his talents. So, would you like to get a cup of coffee and tell me the story about your trip that you must have already told a hundred times?"

3

CHAPTER

SATURDAY MORNING, JEANNIE was already awake when she looked at her alarm clock, which read 7:10. She stretched and thought of Sean, Agent Sean Delaney, and she started to cry. She had lost her fiancé, Ricky Pinheiro, in a gun battle a few years ago and now had been informed that Sean had been killed in an explosion during his recent investigation of the terrorist group Black Cell.

He was an Interpol agent she first met while investigating a group of rogue former military personnel called the Banshees and their leader, Frank Silva, who, together with Dr. Nancy Bell, were planning to steal the actual Ark of the Covenant from a chapel in Ethiopia. The whole investigation blew up in their faces. They later met at the request of Sean, whose agency was stifled over what appeared to be an international sex trafficking ring, only to get involved with modern-day Nazis and their leadership called the Organization.

Shortly after a successful conclusion to their joint investigation, Jeannie was suspended after the Austrian government accused her of murder in their country. It was a bullshit charge orchestrated by the Organization since Jeannie was a kidnap victim and not even armed at the time of the shooting.

She and Sean had already started a romantic relationship and were vacationing at her cabin in Idaho when Sean was assigned a case involving a group of hackers known as the Black Cell. The group made their first appearance on Super Bowl Sunday when they blacked out the championship game's broadcast for several minutes. However, that was just a taster, not their ultimate goal.

They then began liquidating the illegal bank accounts of several elites, particularly targeting corrupt politicians. Next on their agenda were the accounts of both the Democratic and Republican PAC funds. Initially, these funds were secretly deposited with non-profit organizations, but that was just a warmup to their masterpiece, the theft of funds from the largest bank in the world.

To accomplish this, they hacked into various military data banks and appeared to destroy nuclear submarines belonging to the Russians, Chinese, and United States. The world was on the brink of nuclear war when Delaney and his crew eliminated Black Cell, but it resulted in him losing his life.

Weeks went by without any communication from him until Jeannie was notified by Interpol that he had been killed in an explosion in Japan after surviving a shootout with the hackers. They had booby-trapped the entrance to a missile silo they were using as their base of operation.

She couldn't understand why it had taken so long for her to be notified. She could not attend his funeral since he was immediately cremated as he had no family. The whole thing did not make sense. Her inquiries, even with the help of SAC Lomax, were met with resistance. Lomax said he smelled a coverup of some type and told Jeannie she should just let go, which was easier said than done.

Maybe I am one of those people destined to be single for the rest of my life. I mean, my track record involving marriage is pretty sad. My mom and dad, I mean my stepmom and dad, were married for over fifty years. Even my real mom apparently had a great marriage. I really thought Ricky and I would have a family and be together for the rest of our lives, but once again, fate raised its ugly head, and here I am again, alone.

Jeannie threw on her robe after deciding it was going to be a lazy day. She brushed out her hair and put it in a ponytail, only to have several strands fall to the side of her face. After finding her slippers, she went downstairs straight to the dining room.

"Good morning, guys and gals. And how are we this fine Saturday morning?" The koi swam to the surface of their tank, waiting for their food pellets. Jeannie had trained them to eat out of her hand and enjoyed bouncing ideas and thoughts off them. *Bet some shrink would have a field day learning that I discuss investigations with you.*

Her doorbell rang. *Has to be Delores. There goes a quiet and relaxing Saturday.* Sure enough, there she was, the new leader of the neighborhood watch unit who ruled the entire subdivision with an iron hand and a pair of Swarovski binoculars. Nothing got past her, including gossip. If you wanted to know who was having an affair or whose marriage was on the rocks, you just had to ask Delores, and she would give you all the sordid details. *Doesn't every neighborhood have a Delores?*

Jeannie quickly recalled another case that Delores helped solve. It involved a serial killer investigation Jeannie was spearheading with the San Jose Police Department. The killer targeted the elderly and mutilated their bodies after killing them. Delores had commented that when she was a young girl, her aunt and uncle used to employ day laborers when it came time to pick fruit in their orchard. This was something that Jeannie had not thought of, and, sure enough, the killer was an illegal farm worker.

On a scarier note, Delores and her husband had recently received their CCW permits. Knowing Delores was walking around with a Casull .454 caliber handgun gave Jeannie nightmares, but she loved them anyway. Amazing how those two thoughts simultaneously raced through her mind.

"Good morning, Delores. How are you? You look nice today."

"Oh, thank you. I got my hair done yesterday. Do you like the color?" Jeannie almost laughed out loud at the hot pink color with purple highlights Delores had opted for in her new hairdo.

"Well, it is definitely a different look for you. How does Walter like it?"

"Oh, Walter likes it. When I came home after my appointment and walked into the house, Walter could not take his eyes off me. He stared and stared." Jeannie almost lost it and faked a cough to cover an outburst. "You know, Walter is still the romantic. I was going to walk into our bedroom completely naked with my new hairdo, but I thought he might jump my bones," she said, breaking into a loud laugh.

Jeannie felt bad that she always tried to avoid and get rid of Delores, so, to her surprise, she invited her into her front room and said she would bring her a cup of coffee. Delores immediately walked into the dining room and inspected Jeannie's koi. "How are they doing? They seemed okay when I told care of them last time."

"They are doing great. I think I will have to take some of them to my friend's house in a few months since they are getting too big for the tank. I am even thinking of building a koi pond in the backyard. What do you think?"

"Oh, that would be great. Maybe you can get someone to put a gate in the fence between us and Walter and I can come over and enjoy them." Jeannie wasn't too keen on that idea and let it pass.

"So, is anything going on in the neighborhood?" Jeannie asked after giving Delores her coffee.

"Well, get ready for the girl scouts to ring your bell. It's that time of year again. Walter and I always buy too many cookies. He loves those chocolate mint ones, you know. Oh, and Bob and Margaret are going to see the pyramids in Egypt this spring. They asked me and Walter to watch their house while they are gone. Do you know Galina? She's that Russian lady who lives way down on the corner."

"No, I don't know her. Has she been in the United States very long?"

"Oh, gee. Let me think. She has lived in that house for about three years, alone. But now, she and her boyfriend are living together in sin. You know, she was married three times already. From what I heard, she met her boyfriend online and will probably get married again soon. She also has a niece and another young female living with her. Some type of exchange program thing. Let's see, what else? Oh yeah. You will be happy to know that we will not be raising our HOA dues next year. You can thank me for that."

"Well, thank you, Delores. It seemed like they were going up about every two years."

"That's because of that liberal HOA board we had until the neighborhood took it over. Taking ninety days to approve a simple landscaping job was ridiculous. We have it down to fourteen days now."

Saved by the bell, Jeannie thought as her cell rang. "Excuse me, Delores." Jeannie got up and walked to the kitchen with her empty coffee cup. "Loomis."

"Jeannie." It was SAC Lomax. "Two bodies have been found in the grounds of the Presidio. An older female and what might be her daughter. Federal property, so it is ours. Call me later and tell me what we have."

"Gee, I'm sorry again, Delores, but that was my boss. We have another case thrown at us. I need to leave immediately. When I get back, we must continue our conversation."

"Oh my God. I understand. Please be safe."

4

CHAPTER

JEANNIE PICKED ISMAIL up at his house after first saying hi to his wife and family. His wife handed Jeannie some fresh malasadas (Portuguese donuts) and a thermos of hot coffee. Smelling the donuts, she allowed Ismail to drive her Corvette to the Presidio, which he thoroughly enjoyed. "Just watch your speed, Ace. I have a malasada in one hand and a hot cup of coffee in the other."

SFPD uniformed and detectives were at the scene. The area had been taped off. Two of the detectives recognized Jeannie's car and waved them to an area a few yards from the crime scene. "Flores, Loomis. Sorry to have to drag you guys out on a Saturday," said homicide detective Paul Wingate, a twenty-seven-year veteran of the SFPD. "It's a bad one."

Paul and Ismail went way back to when they were involved in tracking down a cop killer striking in the bay area. Back in those days, he was an eager beaver, but with all the "Defund the Police" crap, he just accepts that people die, either naturally or like this, and it is nothing more than just a job. That said, both Ismail and Jeannie knew him as a top-notch homicide investigator and were glad to see him at the scene.

"Jeannie, brushing sugar from her blouse and suit jacket, and Ismail approached an area where two yellow plastic tarps had been placed over the bodies. "So, Paul," Ismail said, "what do we have?"

"Those two joggers over there (pointing to a young male and female in matching green jogging outfits being interviewed by a patrol officer) found the bodies about two hours ago. Looks like they were wrapped in that rug, but after the suspects tossed them down there, the foot of the younger female was sticking out. The male called it in on his cell. Initially, they only saw the younger female, and that is how they called it in. It wasn't until our first uniform got to the scene and took a closer look that we found two of them."

Jeannie lifted the plastic tarp off the younger female while Ismail looked at the other body. "God, someone worked her over. Looks like cut wounds on the body, and the final cause will be her throat being cut. Maybe sixteen to eighteen? No blouse on. Maybe sexual assault. The older female is still fully clothed, but she has a lot of traumas on her face." Ismail said, not expecting a reply.

"That'd be my guess. The older female looks a lot like her, so probably mom and daughter," Jeannie said.

Ismail and Jeannie exchanged positions and looked at the other body.

"Looks like the younger one was tortured more than the older one. Both have ligature marks. Bet they were cuffed facing each other, and the younger one was being cut up to force the older one to talk," Ismail said.

"That's what it looks like to me. Now, the big question, besides who are the pricks that did this to them, is what information were they trying to get?" Paul said.

"Looks like we have our work cut out for us. Thanks, Paul. Our jurisdiction. Lucky us. Is the medical examiner on the way?" Ismail asked.

"Yeah, I called for them once your dispatch said you were almost here. They should be here shortly. I will leave two patrol units here to assist. Just cut them loose when you are through. Happy hunting. Oh, one more thing; love your car, Jeannie."

"Here I was, planning on staying home and sexually harassing my wife while eating hot malasadas, and now, we have a who-done-it double homicide. I sure hope my wife can handle me not taking care of her sexual needs and desires."

"You still haven't seen a therapist about your delusion of grandeur, have you? Your poor wife probably started celebrating your departure as we drove off."

"Very funny. She's probably taking a cold shower and counting the minutes until my return."

"Oh, God. Give me a break." While waiting for the FBI forensic team to arrive, Ismail and Jeannie questioned the medical examiner, Susan Wong, hoping to get more information about the bodies.

"Time of death was approximately nine hours ago. The younger female sustained over twenty-one lacerations, painful but not fatal. The older one had only seven cuts plus the head trauma. Both died due to having their throats cut, leading to blood loss."

"Well, it looks like both were bound by probably plastic cuffs resulting in those ligature marks." Jeannie and Ismail liked Susan Wong. She didn't dilly dally around but went straight to the point, thinking and talking like a cop. "Torture of the young one to influence the older one to talk is my guess. Now, whether the older one gave up what the suspects wanted is your problem."

She looked at Ismail. "Before you ask, my handsome Portuguese stud muffin, I said suspects, but that is only a guess. The older female looks like she was in good shape. Good muscle tone, low body fat. I don't see one person being able to control the situation. No, the way I see it, she was surprised by one suspect, and then a second suspect took control of the teenager. I will put a rush on their prints, and they will be the first ones on the block Monday. Should have something for you by then. Ta ta."

Jeannie knew it was coming. Ismail turned towards her, "Portuguese stud muffin. I'm telling you, boss. When you got it, you got it." Jeannie shook her head and talked briefly with the forensic team upon their arrival before she and Ismail left the scene.

Jeannie dropped Ismail off at his home and then stopped for Chinese takeout around the corner from her Newark home. *Just hope I can get in the house without running into you-know-who.* With the Corvette secured in her garage, she changed into some sweats and sat across from her koi in the dining room. *Got an interesting one. Two tortured females. Possibly mom and daughter. Dumped at the Presidio. Don't have anything to go on yet. Hopefully, something by Monday.*

What she liked about Chinese takeout was the ease of cleaning up afterward. No dishes, pots, or silverware to wash. Everything goes in the trash. She called Lomax and filled him in. Next, a hot bubble bath and a little movie called Loch Ness with Ted Danson and Joely Richardson. What if the Loch Ness monster is not meant to be found was the premise of the film? The last thought on her mind before falling asleep was wondering what information the two victims died for.

***

"What do you mean they did not know about the map? Did you search the house?" asked Klaus Rictner, a sixty-two-year-old German national. His beer belly hung three inches over his pants belt with pubic fat hanging under that. His short, gray crewcut hair only accented his pie face and double chin. His grandfather had been a major in the Waffen-SS, a position that he bragged about often. He even had the SS insignia tattooed under his armpit, listing his blood type in a similar fashion to his grandfather.

"Yes, sir. After they died, Hans and I searched the house twice. There was nothing there except a bunch of old magazines and books, and nothing about the train. If it was there, we would have found it." Erwin Mueller was afraid of Rictner. He knew about his quick temper. In Germany a few years ago, he had seen Rictner slice the throat of one of his subordinates and then laugh as the victim's body twisted and turned on the floor before succumbing to the wound.

"Very well. Keep watching the house. I want it watched 24/7. No one goes in or out without you notifying me. Do I make myself clear?"

"Yes, sir. But we may be here for a long time. I am sure the police will come once they learn the identity of the two females. What do we do when they come?"

"Dummkopf. Let the police do the work for us," Rictner said with a sinister laugh. "Maybe they can find what you two idiots could not."

5

CHAPTER

"GOOD MORNING, BOSS lady," Ismail said before Jeannie could say hello on her cell. We got a hit on the older female's prints. Nola Hetman, fifty-four years old. As the SAC said, she was a full-time federal court interpreter with the administrative office of the US courts here in the city. Nothing on the girl yet."

"Okay, thanks. I'm almost ready for the drive in. See you there." Jeannie gave up trying to speculate on what information a federal court interpreter might have encountered that would lead to her torture and death. Her role meant she was used by both the prosecutor and defense teams in court, putting her in contact with criminal elements. It might be related somehow. She put some cream cheese on a bagel and stirred her coffee. Five minutes to eat and across the Dumbarton she would be.

Ismail met her in the hallway near her office. "Bout time you got here. I thought I would have to move my things back into your office and take command again."

"Fat chance. Did you get any more information on our victim?"

"Due to my extreme talent as a highly-trained FBI agent, I got her home address."

"Good morning, Jeannie," said Darcy, Jeannie's extraordinary IT person. "Ismail, did you get the address and ID on the victim I sent you?" Jeannie just looked at Ismail, whose face turned red as he left, saying he needed another coffee.

"Hi, Darcy. Thanks for the information. You and Burk working on anything interesting?"

"Nah. Just a bunch of paper chases trying to track down offshore accounts for a criminal hedge fund operator. Standard crap."

"Oh well, pays our wages," Jeannie replied. "Depending on what Ismail and I find on the double homicide we inherited, I might need you and Burk." Burk was another great researcher who used technology to its fullest. If you decided to commit a crime and hide, he and Darcy would eventually find you. The rumors in the San Francisco bureau were that both Darcy and Burk were homosexuals but never flaunted it. Over time, however, a few slip-ups by the two revealed that they were romantically involved.

"Anything is better than chasing paper. Just let us know," Darcy said.

Ismail drove Jeannie in his bureau's Crown Vic to a nice subdivision in Half Moon Bay, about twenty-five miles south of San Francisco. A small coastal city in San Mateo County, it had a population of only 12,000 according to the 2020 census. "Maybe we can grab some clam chowder when we get through. Doesn't that sound good? Hot clam chowder with some warm sourdough bread. I can taste it already."

"Do you want more love handles for your wife?"

"More to love, boss lady. More to love." Jeannie smiled. God, she loved her partner.

The home was in the unincorporated community of Princeton-by-the-Sea. "You know, this is where they hold the Mavericks' surfing competition?" Ismail said.

"What did you do? Read Wikipedia last night?" Jeannie asked.

"No. I watch the surfing competitions on TV every year."

"You watch surfing? That's a new one."

"Hey, some of the female surfers are buffed, and sometimes there are bathing suit malfunctions."

"You are a true pervert, my friend. Here we are," Jeannie said, looking at a single-story ranch-style home that looked to be in pretty good condition. The outside walls were decorated with shingles, giving it a New England look, and it was painted in a robin's egg blue color. Like many homes in the Bay Area, nothing was cheap.

After ringing the doorbell several times and then knocking on the door, they decided to take a walk around the perimeter, only to be approached by a neighbor. "They are not home. I haven't seen them since early Saturday morning. My name is Vivian. I live over there." Vivian was in her mid-forties and wearing a straw gardening hat, flannel shirt, a pair of women's jeans, and rubber boots. She began taking off her gardening gloves and continued walking toward the two.

Jeannie showed her badge and introduced herself and Ismail. "Do you know what time on Saturday morning you last saw them?"

"Oh, it was early. Before 8 a.m., for sure. I was getting ready to take my dog to the vet, and I waved as they went by. Is everything alright?"

"We are talking about Nola Hetman, correct?"

"Yes, Nola and her daughter, Anna. This is their house."

"Is Ms. Hetman married?" Ismail asked.

"No, she divorced a long time ago. In fact, she was divorced when the two of them moved in. That was maybe eleven years ago. I never met the husband, and as far as I know, he has never been around for Nola or his daughter."

"Do you know where they were going Saturday?" Jeannie asked.

"Yes. They were going over to Nola's uncle's house in the city to clean it up and get it ready for sale. He died recently, and she inherited the house. Do you think something happened over there?"

"Do you know her uncle's address, by any chance?" Ismail asked, deliberately avoiding her question.

"No, just that it's in San Francisco somewhere, sorry. Nola told me that she and Anna were going to clean up the house Saturday and Sunday and hopefully have it ready for painters right after that. She told me once that it was an old house, but with real estate going through the roof, she was going to get quite a profit from its sale. So, are they okay?"

"No. Unfortunately, Ms. Hetman was the victim of a homicide, and there's a possibility that her daughter was a second victim."

"Oh, my God! Not Nola. Not Anna."

***

"How much longer do we need to sit here and watch a vacant house?" Hans asked Erwin. "There is nothing there. We should be doing something else."

"You have a big set of balls, Hans. Why don't you say that to Rictner? But, before you do, make sure you warn me so I can stand far away from you when he cuts your fuckin' head off."

Hans processed what Edwin said. "Well, you tell me what we are doing here. Even if the police do show up, how will we know if they find anything, huh? Are you going up to them and asking them what they found?" Edwin knew that Hans was all talk and, like a good German, he would do what was necessary to carry out his orders.

"No, asshole. When and if they arrive, we will watch. You understand? I will call Rictner and tell him they are here. Let him decide what we should do. If he fucks up, it is his problem, not ours. I have to take a piss. Give me that paper cup again." Hans gave him the coffee cup, and Edwin almost filled it to the brim. He opened the passenger door and slowly drained it out into the gutter.

Neither he nor Edwin paid any attention to a newer model customized van parked two cars down across the street from them. The van's heavily tinted windows were perfect for the occupants to watch the two Germans.

"Taking another piss," Elijah said to Samuel. The two Mossad agents took turns watching the vehicle across from them. "I might as well take a pee, too," said Samuel, who pulled up a rug from the floorboard, exposing a two-inch hole. He unzipped his pants, and then got on his knees, aiming for the hole. "You know, I am getting pretty good at this. I've only got my pants wet twice."

"I don't have to worry about that since mine's so long it reaches the hole."

"Yeah. Right."

6

CHAPTER

JEANNIE CALLED THE Half Moon Bay Police Department and requested that at least one uniformed officer attend the Hetman address and secure the premises until a team of agents and the FBI forensic team arrived with a telephonic search warrant. Two uniformed officers duly arrived in separate vehicles, one a sergeant.

"FBI, wow. What happened here to bring the feds?" Sergeant O'Callahan asked, reaching out to shake hands with both Jeannie and Ismail. The sergeant with hound dog eyes was older than both of them. His uniform shirt's front pocket was unbuttoned, and they could see a pack of cigarettes inside. He was given a briefing and asked if one uniformed officer could remain until forensics was through with the search of the house. "Not a problem. Old Hank over there loves the overtime, don't you Hank?" Hank, who looked like a rookie, just nodded.

Climbing back into the Crown Vic, Jeannie turned to Ismail. She asked, "Think they will find anything in the house?"

"Hell, I don't know. I am thinking about clam chowder. Okay, okay, just kidding. No, I don't think the murders took place here if that is what you are asking. I think they were killed at her uncle's house or somewhere in between. Depends on whether this was a kidnapping gone bad, and I don't think it was. I hope that Burk and Darcy can find his address. That's where we might get our first break. Now, how about lunch?"

"Alright, gee. Let's find a place to eat. I'll call Lomax and let him know our progress or lack thereof. I also need to get hold of forensics and tell them to look out for an address book or anything that can tell us where the uncle lived. Plus, I need to call Darcy and see what she can find regarding Nola Hetman's bank records, etc. If she finds something, then we can go back and add it to the search warrant."

"I like the way you think, boss."

Jeannie had to admit to herself that the clam chowder and sourdough bread hit the spot, although she would not give Ismail the satisfaction of telling him. Her cell went off. It was Susan Wong from the coroner's office. "Hi, Jeannie. I wanted you to know that the autopsies of both victims will start at 9 a.m. Monday, one right after the other. That's about all I can do for now. Have a nice rest of the weekend."

"After lunch, they returned to their vehicle, Jeannie lost in thought about the murderers.

"Was that Susan? You know she has the hots for me."

"That is wishful thinking on your part. I know I've asked before, but what in the hell does your wife see in you?"

Ismail looked in the rear-view mirror and pointed at himself. "USDA prime. That's what she sees."

Jeannie just shook her head. "Yes, that was Susan Wong. First thing Monday morning, you and I will be observing the two autopsies, so better enjoy tomorrow because I think we will have a busy, busy week. If your wife has some leftover malasadas, can you bring them in?"

After her drive back home from the bureau, Jeannie stopped at a Subway and got a foot-long hot roast beef sandwich, a bag of chips, and a large diet Dr. Pepper. She placed the items on her dining room table and went upstairs to change. Feeling better back in her sweats, she returned to the table with a yellow notepad. She unwrapped the sandwich and tore open the chip bag.

After taking a bite of the foot-long, she made a big circle in the center of the notebook and wrote Hetman Nola/Anna? Placing a chip in her mouth, she looked at her fish. "Okay, guys and girls, this is what I have so far." She drew several other smaller circles on the notepad with lines leading to and from the larger to the smaller ones.

As she finished her sandwich, she looked at her drawing. "What are your thoughts?" she asked. Her koi swam around, occasionally heading to the surface of the aquarium to see if a food pellet had been missed from an earlier feeding. "You guys have given me nothing, but I love you anyway, so here, have some more food." *Maybe I should call Delores and have her and Walter help me solve the case.* She laughed and quickly dismissed the thought.

She slept in until 8 a.m. Sunday and woke feeling refreshed. *Maybe I needed all that sleep after my long cross-country trip.* It was warm enough to leave her bathrobe hanging on the rear of her bedroom door as she made her way down the stairs. Having set the timer on the coffee maker the night before to 7 a.m. Sunday, fresh coffee was waiting, so she poured herself a cup. She grabbed a red potato, an egg, and a quarter link of linguiça and put her frying pan on the burner. She chopped up the potato and put it in the pan with a generous amount of olive oil. While cutting up the linguiça, her thoughts turned to Sean. She noticed she was smiling, thinking about how Ismail had got him hooked on the Portuguese sausage.

While waiting for her breakfast to cook, she called Darcy. "Hope I didn't wake you on this bright and sunny morning." She could hear Burk in the background asking Darcy if she wanted some freshly squeezed orange juice. *Nothing homosexual about those two.*

"No, Jeannie, what's up?"

"When you get in first thing tomorrow, get me everything you can on Nola, including bank records and recent withdrawals, such as might be relevant to and consistent with a possible kidnapping. Then, check her social media accounts and phone records. Oh, and check social media for anything on Anna, just in case."

"Got it. Anything else?"

"Yeah. I don't know how you find a lot of the stuff you find, and I am not going to ask, but we are trying to find Nola's uncle's address. We don't know his name or address, nothing, except that it is somewhere in the city. We are operating on the assumption that she and her daughter were heading over to his place to clean it up for sale. She inherited the property. Right now, we are grasping at straws, so see what you can stir up. Also, pull Burk off his assignment and get him on this with you. Now you owe me for getting you away from your paper chases."

Jeannie wrote a "to-do" list for herself. First was to contact Nola's supervisor and learn whatever she could, including details of her previous and current cases. She would have another agent from her team contact the various high schools in the area to find out where Anna Hetman went to school.

Another action item was to track down the ex-husband. *Don't think he would torture his own daughter, but need to cross all the t's and dot all the i's.* Nola's work file could have the daughter's name as a contact and maybe the ex-husband.

Monday morning and Jeannie was already on the Dumbarton bridge heading to the City by the Bay. The wind was drying her hair as usual as it blew through the cab of her car. She loved the saltwater fragrance as she traveled a dazzling 40 miles an hour or less. She parked her car in the secured parking lot once she arrived at the bureau. She would use her bureau car today if she needed to go out and about.

Lomax had also arrived at the same time so the two rode the elevator up to their floor. "Heard you got an ID on one of the victims. Mother and daughter, you think?"

"We think so. I requested hair samples from the home, so if it comes down to DNA, we would have it. Whatever it was that they would not reveal under torture must be good."

"Drugs?"

"I don't think so. She was a court interrupter, so maybe she got involved in something she could not handle. Don't know yet."

Ismail met the two in the breakroom. As they all nursed their first cups of coffee and solved the world's problems, Darcy and Burk entered. "Good morning, everyone," a bubbly Darcy said. She and Burk each made a cup of green tea. Ismail looked at Jeannie, smiled, and shook his head, muttering, "Millennials."

"We heard that," Burk said.

Lomax excused himself, leaving the four at the table. "Jeannie," Darcy started, "Nola was an only child. She'd been married once and divorced about twelve years ago. She did have one child, and her name is Anna. Forensics stopped by this morning before either you or Ismail got in and dropped off their inventory of stuff taken from the house in Half Moon Bay. They are running DNA from several hairbrushes in what they called 'a teenager's room.' Probably Anna's. There was no evidence of foul play in the house. The teenager did not keep a diary. They did find a phone book, and Burk is going through it." She looked at Burk.

"Very few of the names have listed addresses, so I am using cross directories and something Darcy came up with to help me attach addresses to names. Some are only listed by first or last names. Once I can run what I have through Darcy's system, we might find a match for Nola's uncle's address."

"Damn, I forgot. Ismail, can you put out an APB for Nola's car? It has to be out there somewhere," Jeannie asked.

"Already done, boss. Remember, I'm a highly…" He was cut off by Jeannie before he could finish the sentence with "...trained FBI agent." Everyone laughed. "Okay, good work, Burk, Darcy, and you too, Ace. He and I (pointing to Ismail) have to go to the coroner's office, so we won't be back for several hours. Text me if anything else comes in."

7

CHAPTER

ONE NEWHALL STREET was a more modern building than the FBI office, with two stories above ground and the autopsy and lab rooms in the basement. Jeannie and Ismail showed their IDs to the security guard in the lobby, who was new and did not recognize them. While taking the elevator to the basement, Jeannie pulled out a small vial of Vick's vapor rub and put some under her nose. She offered it to Ismail, who showed her his.

No matter how many times the two of them observed an autopsy, they were never prepared for the smells in the room or the dissection of human bodies. They had talked in the past about how it would probably be easier to see an animal dissected unless it was their own pet.

Susan Wong and her assistant were getting ready to start on Nola. Jeannie and Ismail put on their gowns, surgical hats, and hair and eye protection. "Good morning, agents," Wong said. "Shall we begin?" Not expecting an answer, she pulled a microphone down from the ceiling while her assistant wrote on a handheld whiteboard. The board seemed redundant to Ismail, but it was their standard operating procedure.

Wong described the body as a white female along with her approximate age, weight, and liver temperature at the time of autopsy. She noted that both of Nola's hands had been placed in bags, which she now removed. Each fingernail was scraped, and then the nails were clipped into an evidence bag held by the assistant. A preliminary examination of the body was noted. Nola's hair was examined for residue besides the bloody matted hair. Stab wounds were measured while being photographed. Eventually, a Y-incision was made with the eventual removal of ribs and organs, all being weighed and photographed.

Jeannie jumped when the bone saw was turned on. The skull cap was removed, and Nola's brain was scooped out. It, too, was weighed, sliced, and diced, as Ismail would say, and finally, the first autopsy was complete.

Wong looked at Jeannie and Ismail as she took off her gloves. "Cause of death was massive blood loss after her carotid artery was cut. The other wounds are consistent with cuts that were no doubt painful, but none were life-threatening. I'm going to get a coffee and a bagel before I cut into the next one. Would you like a cup? I buy it online from a company back east. I love their chocolate-flavored brew." Both Jeannie and Ismail joined her.

The second autopsy started fifteen minutes later on what was presumed to be Anna Hetman's body. Wong conducted the autopsy in the exact same manner as before, but it took longer to photograph and measure the wounds due to the number of cuts. "This young lady went through hell," Dr. Wong said. "She was menstruating and received eighteen cut wounds; several were deep, but none struck an artery. The son-of-a-bitch who cut her knew what he was doing. Painful as hell. Neither Nola nor Jane Doe here shows any evidence of sexual penetration. That does not appear to have been the perpetrator's motivation, as far as I can tell.

The cuts on the minor's breasts again seemed to be part of the torture ritual and nothing more. Sorry guys, no smoking gun here to help you solve the case quickly. Like the older female, cause of death was massive blood loss due to throat-cutting."

After throwing their gowns in the solid trash receptacle, Jeannie and Ismail walked toward the elevator. "I am sure glad that neither my mom nor dad had to be butchered like that when they died. I hope to God I will be lucky enough for my doctor to sign off on my cause of death to avoid having to be dissected," Jeannie said. Ismail agreed. She looked at her phone and saw several text messages from Darcy and Burk. She called Darcy. When she finished her call, she looked at Ismail.

"It's starting to come together, Ace. First, they found the high school that Anna attended. A yearbook picture, according to Darcy, matched photos found at the house. DNA from hair samples confirm tentatively that the minor was Anna. Later tests will make it a positive match, but this is enough to assume it was Anna."

"Burk got a possible address for the uncle over near Chinatown. Let's head over there. I can buy you lunch if you're hungry." Ismail was still a little gray around the edges and said he'd pass on lunch. "Poor baby. I thought some veal with red sauce and linguini would make a nice meal." Ismail just glared at her.

Jeannie decided not to call for forensics. She wanted to conduct a preliminary walk-through first. She called legal and requested another rapid telephonic search warrant for the uncle's address. The house was located on Grand Street. Most, if not all, of these homes were connected to each other and built around 1911. Many had been converted into multiple condo units going in the millions of dollars if you wanted to purchase one.

Parking, as in most of San Francisco, was at a premium, and Ismail had to park several houses down from the residence. "You know, even if this place is a dump inside, Hetman was going to get a lot of money from its sale," Jeannie said.

"Yeah. And look at all the Chinese restaurants within walking distance."

"Oh, now you're hungry?"

Hans hit Erwin's leg, waking him up. "We have two people walking toward the house. What should we do?" Erwin straightened up and looked at the residence, seeing a blond woman and Hispanic male climbing the five steps to the front door. "Got to be the cops. Now what?"

"Let's see what they do first, and then I will call Rictner," Erwin said, digging his cell out of his pocket.

Ismail rang the front doorbell and then proceeded to knock, not getting a response to either. Jeannie tried the door, but it was locked. Jeannie climbed back down the steps and, after shading her eyes, looked up toward the roof. The façade had a fire escape ladder connecting from the ground level all the way up to the fourth floor. "Lot of house for one person," Jeannie observed.

"Yeah, it is. You know, I heard on the news a little while ago that many of these older multi-storied houses are owned by a bunch of slumlords who divide each floor into two to three units and charge people three to four thousand dollars a month to live in them. Hell, the size of this place, a slumlord could make twelve rooms easily and draw in some serious change," Ismail observed.

"It's nuts. I heard the same story, and they interviewed someone who was renting a unit for $3,000 a month. He justified paying that much to live in a walk-in closet-sized room as being more convenient than commuting back and forth each day from Walnut Creek, plus having to pay the bridge fare or BART ticket prices. He gets off work, calls an Uber, and is home in fifteen minutes. Each floor shares a bathroom, and there is a designated area that is supposed to act as a kitchen, but it only has a small honor's bar type refrigerator and a hot plate."

"So," Ismail asked. "What do you want to do? I can force my way in if you want."

"No. I have a bad feeling about this whole case, and if we screw up along the way, we might jeopardize the investigation. Call SFPD and have them send over a patrol car to watch the place until we get a search warrant. I'll go back to the car and get some crime scene tape."

Within twenty minutes, two SFPD units arrived at the residence. They put on their yellow caution lights and doubled park. No parking problem for them. "Hi, Flo, how's it hanging?" asked Sergeant Tom Hale. "Haven't seen the FBI's finest since that big shootout at the bar where those two officers were killed. Nice job tracking down the killer and putting him down. Saved the taxpayers of this fucked up city some money."

Ismail introduced Jeannie, who asked him about the possibility of having one of his officers secure the residence due to the possibility of it being a crime scene until their forensic team arrived with a search warrant. Sergeant Hale said that would not be a problem. He talked with the other uniformed officer, shook hands with Ismail and Jeannie, and left. "Sorry to tie you up with this," Jeannie said to the officer, now stuck at the scene.

"Not a problem. Gives me time to catch up on reports. Do you want me to stay once they get here? No problem, if you do."

"That would be great if you could. Don't know if a lot of looky-loos will show up once the search team arrives. Once they get here, they will notify us, and we will return."

***

"What are they doing?" Rictner asked Erwin.

"No one answered the door. Of course, we expected that. They must have called the San Francisco Police Department because one is parked at the front of the residence, but the other two left."

"I bet they went to get a search warrant. Call me when they return." Elijah turned to Samuel. "Things are about to get interesting, I think."

8

CHAPTER

THEY DECIDED TO have lunch at the Oriental Pearl restaurant on Clay Street. Ismail ordered broccoli beef, while Jeannie had pork chow mein with pan-fried noodles. "Hope we get lucky inside the house," Jeannie said while adding soy sauce to her noodles.

Ismail agreed as he attacked a large broccoli floret. "I have a feeling it's the crime scene, and the assholes who killed them have probably already tossed the place looking for whatever. Can I ask you a question without you being offended?"

"Gee. After all these years working together and all the harassment, now you are worried about offending me?" Jeannie asked while smiling. "Go ahead, and I promise I won't shoot you."

"Okay. How are you handling Delaney's murder? I know you two were starting to get close and all. I mean, the whole shooting, explosion, and investigation all seem to be so hush-hush. Know what I mean?"

Jeannie waited until she had taken a sip of her hot tea. "Sure, his death hurt me, and I still think about him, but not in the same way as your cousin's death. I was in love with Ricky. Hell, we were engaged when those assholes shot him in Concord." She choked up and swallowed. "Maybe the hurt wasn't as bad since we had only been together for a short time, but, I agree, Interpol has really put a lid on his killing and the whole Black Cell thing. Even Lomax, with all his contacts, hasn't been able to learn anything other than the bullshit Interpol has released."

"You know, I went to his office in the city to see if maybe I could learn more from the staff there. Everyone was new. Delaney's whole staff had been reassigned. I even had Darcy do some off-the-books snooping, and she came up with nothing."

Just before they paid the bill, Jeannie received a text. She read it and looked at Ismail. "Forensics are at the residence. Let's go and check it out."

Erwin looked at Hans. "Give me those binoculars. There are a bunch of people at the house. They are putting on white protective gear and are preparing to go in. One has a crowbar. Yes, they just forced the door open, and they are all going in. No, I have not seen the first two officers. Okay, I will call you in a few minutes. Rictner wants us to report once they start taking anything out of the house."

Ismail parked behind the SFPD vehicle and turned on the small rear yellow light in the back of the Crown Vic. They both put on booties and plastic gloves and FBI windbreakers before entering the ground floor. A technician had already placed several numbered placards on the floor near bloody footprints.

"Yep. This is where it all began," Ismail said before they both began climbing the stairs. The walls badly needed a paint job and had several large cracks. The rug was probably over forty years old. It was almost as if they were walking back in time.

"Jesus. I am surprised this place held up during the Loma Prieta earthquake. Did you feel the sway on the stairs as we were climbing? I hope the big one doesn't happen today," Ismail said. Jeannie did not respond. They reached the first floor, where most of the activity was taking place.

On the kitchen floor were two large spots of coagulated blood next to two chairs. The forensic supervisor saw Jeannie and approached her. "Hi, Jeannie. This one's yours?" asked Marsha Mays, a tall Black woman who was easily 5'10". She had piercing jade green eyes and a dynamite smile. She and her technicians were dressed in what Ismail called their Pillsbury Dough Boy suits.

Afraid so, Marsha. As you see, I brought my little buddy."

"Of course. Your egotistical Portuguese partner," she said, looking at Flores with a flirtatious smile. "As you can see, this appears to be where your two victims were killed. The chairs show signs of them fighting the plastic cuffs, which are now lying in those pools of blood. We haven't found any knives that were the murder weapons, so they must have taken them when they left.

"Over there (pointing to what was the dining room), it looks like they pulled up a throw rug as you can see how the old carpet is faded. The rug the victims were found in at the Presidio will probably match the size of the square there, and we will see if the blood matches.

"The rest of the house has been tossed. We haven't found any blood transfers except down here and on the steps going down to the entrance. Looks like someone stayed down here with the two victims while the other searched the upper two floors. It's a mess."

Jeannie thanked Marsha and her team and explored the next two floors. As Marsha said, the contents of the rooms were thrown about. Bookcases were turned over, and two beds had their mattresses turned upside down. A goldfish had seen better days and was lying on the floor next to his bowl. "What do you think?" Ismail asked.

"I don't think they found what they were looking for and took it out on the Hetmans. Also, I don't think Nola knew the whereabouts of what they wanted, as she would have given the information up to save her daughter. How that speculation is going to help us, I don't know. Let's go back to Marsha."

Jeannie instructed Marsha to secure the scene with tape once they had wrapped things up. Marsha was to text her if they found anything important after they left, but Jeannie wasn't holding her breath. "Let's go back to the office. I need a cup of coffee, and we can bring Burk and Darcy up to speed."

9

CHAPTER

JEANNIE WAS EXCEPTIONALLY quiet on the drive back to the bureau. "You alright, boss?"

"Yeah. What did you think of the house?"

"I think it is going to take some serious coin to get rid of all the blood and shit from the floor in the kitchen, not to mention a major refacing of the walls and ceilings. I have never seen so many cracks. It's also going to take lots and lots of paint. Is that what you mean?"

"Maybe that's it, but something seems off. I can't put my finger on it. I just had this weird feeling as we walked through each floor. Oh well, we can go back later after forensics are through. If not today, then before we release the crime scene."

"The two cops showed up again but didn't stay too long. They just left. No, they left with nothing. The lab people, or whoever they are, didn't take much from the house. It doesn't look like they found anything, either. Okay, we will wait for them."

"That was Rictner. Klauss and Carl will be here soon to relieve us. Finally, we get a break. He wants us to return tomorrow morning. We are to work out a schedule with them when they arrive."

"Good. I need to take a shit and sitting here all this time is bad for my hemorrhoids. I think I grew a few more," Hans said, stretching himself.

***

"Gabriel, the first set of Germans have left, and now there is a new team here. The crime scene people have packed up and gone. The two FBI agents have also gone. They did not appear to have taken anything with them. If the item is in the house, it doesn't seem to have been found. Okay, yes, we will leave now and return in the morning." Elijah turned to Samuel. "Let's get out of here."

Jeannie checked in with her secretary and then Lomax, bringing him up to speed. Ismail got a hold of Darcy and Burk, and the rest of the team, telling them to meet in the large briefing room in thirty minutes.

"Hey, Darcy said she and Burk came up with a lot of new information and will present it to the group, so maybe we will see some light at the end of the tunnel," Ismail said to Jeannie as he met her in the hallway near the bathrooms.

"Let's hope so. Right now, I feel like a Ferrari spinning circles on an oil-slicked road, spending a lot of energy but not showing any forward progress."

Marsha had been invited to present first-hand what, if any, results had come back from her forensic team's search of the house. Ismail had made sure there was a fresh pot of coffee ready for everyone and hot water for tea. At 2 o'clock, Jeannie was ready to get the ball rolling.

"Marsha, why don't you go first since I know you are extremely busy." Marsha got up in front of everyone and opened her leather binder. She took out a single piece of paper and laid it on the table.

"I already shared some of this with some of you, but I'll go over it again. Blood found on the kitchen floor, etc., was matched to your two victims. We gathered up a lot of trace evidence, but most of it is coming back to the owner of the house. The suspects must have worn gloves since the prints we have processed all come back to the owner and the two victims.

Your suspects really did a number on trashing the place. We examined all the books thrown on the floor and found nothing of interest. I wish I had more, but there was nothing there to tie your potential suspects to the scene once you catch them."

"Thanks, Marsha," Jeannie said while looking at Burk and Darcy. They waited for Marsha to gather up her stuff before moving up to the front of the group. Burk went first.

"Franz Detwrick, the owner of the house, died a few weeks ago. He was 101 years old. He was born and raised in Hamburg, Germany. He had one brother and one sister; both died in the bombings of the city toward the end of World War II. His wife died back in the early 1960s. She originally came from Hamburg also. There are no known children." Burk looked at Darcy, who took over.

"He had an interesting past, to say the least. This guy was a cold-blooded Nazi of the worst kind. I'm surprised he lived long enough to celebrate his 101st birthday, but I'll come back to that. We haven't had a chance to really look into his finances. It appears that he has been living off a pension and social security, but we think there is something fishy. I can't believe that a damn Nazi gets our social security. Anyway, he was an SS officer, reaching the rank of lieutenant. It looks like his biggest asset was the equity in his home, which has been paid off for some time. Where he came up with the money is another area that needs to be investigated. He hasn't had a driver's license for over thirty years. No criminal record once he got to the US, but he was a convicted murderer, in my opinion."

Just then, SAC Lomax entered the briefing room. "Don't let me stop you. Please, continue," he said while filling his coffee cup. "As I said, he was a Nazi. He held the rank of lieutenant in the SS, and it looks like his first assignment was at an extermination camp called Sobibor. I think I pronounced it right."

"You did, Darcy. In my opinion, for the short time it was in operation, it was worse than Auschwitz-Birkenau. Sorry for interrupting," Lomax said, sipping his coffee.

"Not at all, sir. Perhaps you can help fill in some additional information after I am through? Franz Detwrick served a little over a year at the death camp and was then transferred back to Germany, where his trail seems to have gone cold until he was captured while trying to escape near the bunker where Hitler killed himself. When he was seized, he was wearing a non-ranking officer's uniform, but an SS tattoo was found under his armpit, indicating that he was, in fact, an SS officer."

One of the younger agents from Jeannie's team, Agent Paula Delgado, asked out loud, "Why get tattooed in the armpit? I mean, who's going to see a tattoo there?" Ismail thought to himself, *another damn Millennial.*

Everyone turned to Lomax, who took another sip of coffee before answering. "The tattoos didn't say SS. Members of the Waffen-SS wore them to identify their blood group. After the war, the tattoo was taken as prima facie evidence of being part of the Waffen-SS, leading to potential arrests and prosecutions. I'm more interested in learning why he was at the Führerbunker."

"Why's that, sir?" Burk asked.

"As you may or may not know, since you are all too damn young (everyone laughed), by that time, the war had turned against Nazi Germany. Hitler refused to leave for a more secure place or even leave the country. Some of the Nazi hierarchy wanted him to travel to Austria, or even South America, in one of their U-boats. But he wanted to stay in Berlin, initially thinking that his military prowess could rally his remaining troops and turn the tide back against the Allies."

"But things continued to grow worse. The reason I am curious about your subject being arrested in that location is that most people in the Führerbunker were higher-ups in the Nazi organization. Most left before the Russians arrived, each hoping to make a deal to keep themselves out of prison for war crimes. I guess he could have been there as part of the SS guards protecting Hitler."

"Huh," Burk said. He turned to Darcy, but she told him to continue. "Again, we still have a lot of research to conduct, but suffice to say, he was arrested and identified as an officer of the SS. He was eventually tried and convicted for war crimes in Nuremberg and given a sentence of thirty years, which he served."

"Wait a minute. He was assigned to Sobibor? Was he one of those who did not receive the death penalty?" Lomax asked.

"That's correct, sir. He did his full sentence at Spandau Prison. Again, Darcy and I have not had enough time to get more information about his wartime activities and incarceration, but we will work on it. We also have not yet investigated his finances."

Everyone turned again towards Lomax. "Shortly after the war ended, the four powers, France, Great Britain, Russia, and the United States held a series of war crime trials in Nuremberg, the place where Hitler held a lot of his propaganda rallies. The initial trials were held for the remaining elites of the Nazi party who had been captured or turned themselves in. Himmler had been captured but committed suicide, the same as Hitler and Goebbels."

"Hermann Goering, Hitler's number two, Albert Speer, Hitler's chief architect, Alfred Jodl, chief of operations, and Wilhelm Keitel, commanding chief of the Wehrmacht, to name a few, stood trial. From November 1945 to October 1946, if memory serves, twenty-one defendants were adjudicated. Nineteen were convicted, and three were acquitted."

"Of those convicted, twelve were sentenced to death. Three defendants were sentenced to life imprisonment, and four to prison terms ranging from ten to thirty years. On October 16th, I believe, executions were carried out by hanging in the gymnasium of the courthouse.

Hermann Goering committed suicide the night before his execution. Somehow, he got a hold of a cyanide capsule. In 1947, the prisoners sentenced to incarceration were sent to Spandau Prison in Berlin, which, as you say, is where your suspect did his time."

"The reason I am surprised your subject was not executed is that, as I said, Sobibor was built purely as an extermination center. The war was turning against Germany, and Hitler knew that time was running out to eliminate all the Jews in Europe. He even re-routed some of his trains away from the war effort to the transportation of Jews to Sobibor, Treblinka, and Belzec.

As sick as it sounds, there was a competition between the three camps to see who could offload their human transports and get them into the gas chambers and then to the crematoriums the quickest. It became a numbers game." Jeannie heard Burk whisper, "Jesus," to Darcy.

"There were about fifty SS, Austrian, and Ukrainian guards assigned to Sobibor. These were some of the most sadistic human beings you can imagine. With a small number of Jews selected and allowed to live and supply services to the SS and the camp, the rest of the transported Jews headed to the assembly line leading to death. The camp was in operation for only a year-and-a-half, but during that time, an estimated 170,000 to 250,000 people were murdered."

"The camp ceased operations after a prisoner revolt that took place in October 1943. The plan was a long shot for the Jews and Russian POWs who helped in the escape attempt. It involved two phases. In the first phase, teams of prisoners were to discreetly assassinate each of the SS officers. In the second phase, all 600 prisoners would assemble for the evening roll call and walk to freedom out of the front gate.

However, the plan was disrupted after only eleven of the SS officers had been killed. The prisoners had to escape by climbing over barbed wire fences and running through a minefield under heavy machine gun fire. About 300 prisoners made it out of the camp, of whom 58 are known to have survived the war. After the escape, Himmler ordered the camp to be razed and planted a bunch of pine trees over its location. Sorry for taking up your time. That's what happens when you are a history nut." No one spoke for several seconds.

"Oh, my God," Darcy said. "Please, sir, is there more you can share?"

"There were three trials for the Sobibor guards and most perpetrators of Operation Reinhart, the final solution to the Jewish question, but many were never brought to trial. Only a few received the death penalty, as hard as that is to believe. I guess that worked in your subject's favor. If you like, Jeannie, I can track down more information about him if someone can give me his particulars. Sounds like your team has other avenues to explore."

"That would be great, sir," Jeannie replied.

Agent Delgado leaned over and whispered a question to Jeannie, “How does the SAC know all this stuff? He isn’t that old, is he?”

Jeannie suppressed a laugh and said, “No. As he said, he is a history buff.”

“Damn, they never taught us about this stuff in school,” she replied.

“There you go,” Jeannie said while looking at Ismail, who was wondering what the world was coming to.

Jeannie got back up in front of her team. “Alright. Let’s call it a day. I am authorizing you to go home early and beat the commute. I want everyone here by 9 a.m. tomorrow. I will work up your assignments regarding this case and hand them out after the morning briefing. If you have active cases, see if you can hand them off to someone. If you need help, let Ismail know, and he will decide what to do. I don’t know where this case is going to take us, but since it all seems to be related to a Nazi animal, I don’t think we are going to have a smooth ride.”

10

CHAPTER

JEANNIE, AS WAS customary, made copies of photographs of the two victims and a picture Darcy had dug up of the mysterious Franz Detwrick, wearing his SS uniform, to take home and display on her upstairs spare bedroom wall. She stopped at her local chipotle Mexican grill and ordered a burrito bowl to go. Once home, after feeding her fish and telling them about her day, she went upstairs with the material from work and placed it on her desk.

She changed out of her work clothes into her sweats and went downstairs to the kitchen to get her dinner and a diet soda before returning to her upstairs study. In between bites, she hung the items on her whiteboard. She pulled out an eight-and-a-half by eleven yellow notepad and began writing down what they knew so far, followed by action items. She would add some of this information to the whiteboard later.

- Nola Hetman - fifty-four years old - Federal Court Interpreter with the Administrative Office of the US Courts. Only heir to estate of Detwrick.
- Anna Hetman – seventeen years old. Daughter of Nola. High school student.
- Franz Detwrick – 101 years old – deceased. Uncle to Nola – SS Lt.
- Sobibor death camp and later ????

Action items:

- Interview Hetman's supervisor(s) and co-workers.
- Review cases she was involved in.
- Location of her car.
- Search residence again for communications with Detwrick.
- Conduct interviews with Anna's friends (school, etc.).
- Check social media accounts for all and their computers.
- Complete background on Detwrick (SAC will focus on war crimes and career with Waffen SS).
- Phone records of all persons.
- Safe deposit box(s) belonging to Detwrick and Nola.
- Interview Detwrick's neighbors.
- Confirm no other relatives.

- Conduct additional search of his residence.

Jeannie made herself a cup of coffee and reviewed her action items, making team assignments to be distributed the next day. *Going to take a lot of time,* she thought as she headed off to bed.

Berlin

"Gentlemen, please be seated," said Otto Heiliger, leader of the Organization, a worldwide conglomerate of individuals dedicated to the rise of the Fourth Reich. Standing in front of a large auditorium with both the SS and Nazi swastika flags behind him, he waited for everyone to sit down. There he stood, in his freshly-pressed black SS uniform and highly shined boots. Clean-shaven and with black hair combed over to his left side, his blue eyes scanned the crowd before him.

The Organization hierarchy consisted of high-ranking SS officers, carrying on the traditions and customs that were established by Henrich Himmler going back to 1925, including wearing the uniform with the death head insignia on special occasions like today. Most members were CEOs, CFOs, and leaders of major international businesses, as well as occupying high-level positions inside various governments. Society had no knowledge about modern-day Nazis holding such important positions of power in their countries, including the United States.

"Let's proceed. I know many of you are skeptical about the existence of a map and diary that will lead us to our Führer's gold train. Articles like this can only add to your skepticism." He holds up a newspaper with the headlines, *Researchers Claim of the Discovery of Hitler's Secret Gold Train Debunked."* People in the audience began having their own conversations, which Heiliger allowed for a minute before calling for their attention again.

"Yes, although they did find one additional tunnel near Ksiaz castle, geologists found no train. A few of you have been made privy to actions we are taking regarding the whereabouts of this train, so today, the council and I believe it is time to reveal that information to the entire Organization. The operation we have in progress is in San Francisco, California."

Heiliger looked at an SS officer behind a small desk with an opened laptop. The officer took his glance as an order to display the first article on a large side screen. "This is a picture of Lt. Franz Detwrick. I am afraid Detwrick passed away a few weeks ago, at the age of 101. Detwrick, shown here with Reichsmarschall Goering giving him a medal at Sobibor, was placed in charge of the transportation logistics of our Führer's wealth, his gold train, to ensure the rise of the Fourth Reich." Several people shouted, "Heil Hitler!" Heiliger raised his hand for silence.

"From our intelligence apparatus going back many, many years, we have chased many rabbits down their rabbit holes, as the Americans say. We now know that many of these rumors are just that. We have spent too much money trying to track down these trains. Yes, I said trains, since we do know that Reichmarschall Goering ordered several trains to be loaded with valuables in different parts of not only the Fatherland but also countries that were later occupied by the Allies."

"From our intelligence, Lt. Detwrick was a very secretive man, having few friends in the SS. This could be related to his rapid rise in rank or, perhaps, the perceived favoritism he received from the reichmarschall. Who knows?" We believe that Detwrick siphoned some of the riches off for his personal gain, along with recorded transactions of the Reich during the construction of the tunnel containing one of the trains.

Our agents conducted a search of his home after his death but were unsuccessful in finding a diary or maps that would aid us in finding the treasure. Recently, the American FBI was observed also searching his home. To date, it appears they have also found nothing."

Max Fisher, a high-ranking member of the Organization, raised his hand. Upon receiving recognition, he stood. "I have two questions. Many of us here have also heard rumors that Martin Bormann ordered several U-boats to be loaded with wealth from the Third Reich and sent them to Argentina. Are we attempting to locate these U-boats? Second, regarding our operation in San Francisco, what are we going to do if the American FBI finds the documents we seek?" Without hesitation, Heiliger responded.

"The Organization has spent an exhaustive amount of time and research regarding the rumors of Bormann ordering U-boats to South America. I can tell you that from this research, every U-boat has been accounted for, and no treasures have been found. Now, to answer your second question about what we are going to do if the American FBI finds the documents we seek, that is an easy answer. We will take them from them."

11

CHAPTER

JEANNIE AND ISMAIL met Shirley Lawson at the federal court building early the next morning, before court started. An older woman with short gray hair, very close to retirement, in Jeannie's estimation, was still in shock after learning that Nola and her daughter had been murdered. "She was the nicest, most loving person. If someone wasn't feeling well, she would offer to cover their shift. Why would anyone want to hurt her?"

"Ms. Lawson, can you tell me what type of case Nola has been working on recently?" Jeannie asked.

"Oh, the one she is on now has more twists and turns than a diamondback rattler. It involves the Russian Organized Crime family. Nola was fluent in Russian as well as Ukrainian. I think only one of the defendants spoke a little English, so Nola interpreted the proceedings for them." Ismail and Jeannie looked at each other.

For the next twenty-plus minutes, she gave a synopsis of the case to date. Afterward, she searched her memory but could not think of any other high-profile case that Nola had been involved in. Ismail and Jeannie thanked Lawson and headed back to the bureau, where Jeannie called part of her team together, including her IT gurus, Darcy and Burk.

Okay, everyone. Ismail and I just got back from interviewing Nola's supervisor at the federal courthouse. One of Nola's recent cases involved the Drug Enforcement Agency (DEA), homeland security, and the Russian Organized Crime family. The ROC had a plan to use a Russian-built submarine to smuggle cocaine from Colombia to the United States, dropping the drugs off on the coast of San Diego and up here in San Francisco. But this was only supposed to be the start of their global criminal alliance.

The ROC also involved itself with the Sicilian Mafia, the 'Ndrangheta, the Camorra, the Boryokudan (Japanese Yakuza), Chinese Triads, Korean criminal groups, Turkish drug traffickers, and Colombian drug cartels, along with other South American drug organizations, all liking the idea of using Russian subs for not only the transportation of narcotics but also for money laundering and counterfeiting.

"Jesus Christ! It's like the New World Order of criminals!" Burk exclaimed, laughing.

"The Russian submarine was loaded in Colombia on the border with Ecuador with cocaine, morphine, and fentanyl. They sailed with a minimum crew to allow more space for the drugs. Just as they approached San Diego, a fire broke out on the sub," Jeannie said, turning the presentation over to Ismail.

"After putting out the fire, they still had to surface to vent the boat. They were spotted by a Lockheed P-3 Orion, which reported their sighting to the Coast Guard. The fire had damaged their controls. There was no time to start unloading their cargo onto lifeboats as saving themselves was more important. In other words, they had two choices. Go down with the boat, drugs and all, or surrender. For some reason, the case ended up here in San Francisco federal court, where Nola was used for her interpreting skills. According to her supervisor, the case is on hold since allegations arose of an attempt to tamper with jurors with offers of money for their not guilty vote when it went to deliberation."

"There's a motive for you," Darcy said.

"You think maybe Nola was also targeted by the ROC? I don't know what influence she could have on the jury. Maybe they wanted her to do something else," Agent Tomson asked from the back row.

"Let's think about that," Jeannie answered. "She is in the courtroom during the whole trial, but she really can't go up to individual jurists without being noticed by everyone in the room. And that would include trying to pass notes," Jeannie said, not expecting a reply.

"But what if she somehow got insider information about the prosecutor's or defense's case and was feeding it to the opposite party?" Burk offered.

"Well, that's a possibility, but why kill her and her daughter?" Darcy asked. Lomax entered the breakroom to refill his coffee cup and see if there was anything to eat and overheard the brainstorming taking place.

"Maybe they didn't intend to kill anyone, but someone got carried away in slapping them around. I mean, Nola gets killed in the process, and now they need to silence her daughter."

Everyone chewed on his remarks. "Darcy, go back and look at Nola's bank records. See if there have been any strange deposits into her account. I doubt that her daughter had an account but check anyway. Ismail, we need to go interview those assholes in jail and see if we can get any information from them. They are lawyered up, but since we know they could not have done the murders, maybe we can convince their attorneys that we just want to chat and that they won't face any new charges. Okay, everyone. Let's get going.

After a phone call with the lead ROC attorney, Jeannie had the legal department send him a copy of an agreement regarding interviewing several key defendants with a promise of no new indictments. A copy was faxed to his office, and once received, he called to accept the terms. Copies were also made for the signatures of the defendants in custody.

Ismail offered to drive since lunch was promised afterward. They parked in an open "reserved for law enforcement vehicle" slot and entered the jail. They were escorted to a small interview room by a deputy who asked which of the inmates they wanted to see first?"

"Let's start off with Maxim Sidorov," Jeannie said, looking at her list."

"Got it," Deputy Morris said. "By the way, his attorney is coming down the hallway."

"Why did you choose Sidorov?" Ismail asked.

"He was the captain of the Russian submarine."

"Agent Loomis? I'm Brett Blackstone, the lead attorney for the group." Blackstone was wearing an easily $3,000 dark blue tailored suit with a lighter blue satin shirt and sporting cufflinks made of gold with scarlet inserts. A gold satin tie finished the ensemble. He offered his hand to Jeannie, who shook it. "Thank you for the agreement letter. I hope my presence here is okay with you. These individuals can be hard to deal with at times."

"Not at all, and we expected you to be here. Makes it nice and clean in court if things go sideways. This is my senior agent, Ismail Flores." The two shook hands as they heard the door being opened.

Sidorov entered the room and shook hands with Blackstone while looking at Ismail and Jeannie, especially Jeannie. He was the thinnest and smallest Russian Jeannie had ever seen. Maybe his height of 5'2" made his selection easy as part of the submarine crew. He had a traditional short haircut and mousy eyes. Jeannie thought, *can't believe this fucker was the captain of the sub.*

"Maxim, this is Agent Loomis and Agent Flores of the FBI. They are not here to question you in any way about the charges against you or the others. I have a signed agreement to that fact. I believe you have a form for Maxim?" Blackstone asked Jeannie.

"Yes. She pulled the form from a folder and slid it across the table to Blackstone. She realized that he was speaking to Sidorov in English. "If you can get your client to sign at the bottom, we can start." Blackstone glanced at the document and recognized that it was a duplicate of the one he had been provided earlier. Now changing to Russian, and while looking at Sidorov, he handed him a pen telling him to sign. Jeannie, who understood and spoke fluent Russian, just smiled at Ismail, who knew she understood the conversation taking place.

Sidorov had a smirk on his face as he leaned forward toward Jeannie. "Are you sure you are not here for my conjugal visit request?" he asked in English.

Blackstone put his hand on Sidorov's forearm, which Maxim threw off. "Can't a man make a joke?" he asked and then began to laugh while leaning back in his chair. "What do two members of the FBI want with me? You feds have already made fuckin' false charges and want to put me away for a long time." He tried, unsuccessfully, to lean the chair further back, and gave up.

"Mr. Sidorov. As this paper says, we are not here to bring new charges against you stemming from the incident with the submarine you were found in."

"That is a lie. I was not in a submarine. I was in the water, and a submarine stopped to rescue me." Ismail coughed while covering his mouth. Blackstone looked at Jeannie and just shrugged his shoulders.

"Whatever," Jeannie responded. "What my partner and I want to ask you pertains to a person that was always in the courthouse with you and your friends, the other defendants." He looked puzzled, then glanced at Blackstone. Jeannie pulled a photograph of Nola from her file and slid it to Blackstone, who, after examining it, slid it to Maxim.

"Who is this bitch?" he asked while holding the picture.

"Her name is Nola. She was the court interrupter and was in the court every time you and the other defendants were present."

"If you say so. But what has that got to do with me? She is too ugly for my taste, but you? Now we are talking."

While looking at Blackstone, Jeannie asked another question, anticipating his objection. "Mr. Sidorov, do you know anything about someone trying to influence the jurors in your case?"

Surprisingly, Blackstone did not object to the question.

"Miss FBI lady, do you know who I work for?" Blackstone again immediately placed his hand on Maxim's forearm, but this time he did not pull it away.

"Yes. You are part of the Russian Organized Crime family. Is that supposed to impress me?" Jeannie replied.

"I have a big dick that will impress you," he said as he leaned forward, laughing uncontrollably. Jeannie looked at Ismail, who got up and notified the deputy that they were through with Sidorov.

Artyom Vasiliev was taller than the submarine captain. Maybe five feet six, but just as skinny, with tattoos covering his neck and arms. He sat in his seat and folded his arms across his chest, and just looked at Blackstone, not at Ismail or Jeannie.

In Russian, Blackstone gave Vasiliev the names of both agents. He was then shown a document like the one signed by Sidorov and told to sign. "My client only speaks Russian," Blackstone said. If you ask me your questions, I will translate and do the same with his responses."

Jeannie smiled at Ismail. "That would be fine," she replied. In English, she again repeated the terms and conditions of the agreement document, and Blackstone repeated to Vasiliev in Russian pretty much everything she said, word for word. "Mr. Vasiliev, do you know this person?" showing him Nola's picture. Blackstone repeated the question.

Artyom looked at Jeannie, then the photograph, and, in Russian, reported back to Blackstone that he only knew her as a woman who was always in the courtroom and could speak Russian. He added that he had never talked to her and didn't know her name. He then asked why.

Blackstone repeated his response but did not add his question. Jeannie smiled and answered in Russian that Nola and her daughter had been murdered and asked what he knew about their murders.

Blackstone had a surprised look on his face. "You speak Russian?" Vasiliev asked.

"Dah," Jeannie said. She asked a few more questions in his native language but could tell that even Ismail realized this was going to be a dead end.

The interviews with Mikhail Kovlov and Ivan Orlov confirmed that they knew nothing about Nola or her murder. The ROC was not involved in their double homicide investigation. "Your Russian is excellent,

Agent Loomis. Where did you learn it?" Blackstone asked as they were wrapping up the final interview.

"My next-door neighbor was from Belarus, and she taught me as I was growing up. She was a stickler and made sure that I spoke like a native. I once traveled to Minsk, Moscow, and St. Petersburg, and most people there were surprised that I could speak it like a native. I don't get to use it much anymore unless I'm watching a foreign film."

"Well, boss lady. What do you think?" Ismail asked while they walked back to their vehicle.

"I don't think these guys had any involvement in the murders. I think the youngest one, Ivan, would have given up his mother to get out of jail. Oh well, it was a rabbit hole we had to check out. Let's go and get lunch."

"Now you're talking. I know a great place about a block away."

12

CHAPTER

LOMAX HAD MADE it back to his desk with his second cup of coffee and a bagel when his desk phone rang. The clock on his wall read 11:30 a.m. "Sir, there are two individuals here in the lobby who wish to speak to you. They have both presented identification as being with the Israeli government. Would you like them to be escorted to your office?"

"Yes, send them down."

Ariel Segal appeared to be the leader of the two individuals. She entered as Lomax stood. *Probably in her early forties*, Lomax thought. She had short brown, collar-length hair with matching eyes. She only had small stones in her earlobes, and he could detect the slight odor of her perfume, which he liked. Dressed in a dark pants suit with a lighter-colored jacket and a white blouse, she extended her hand and introduced herself. She then introduced Levi Cohen, who also shook the SAC's hand.

He appeared to be much younger than Segal. Thick black hair and brown eyes that scanned Lomax's office. He was dressed in business casual with a pullover, blue short-sleeved shirt, and brown pants. "Agent Lomax, we apologize for not requesting an appointment to see you," Segal said.

"Please, take a seat," Lomax answered, motioning to two chairs opposite his desk.

"I understand you are both representing the State of Israel. Is that correct?"

"That is correct. I am sure your agency will do verification checks on us, so let us speed up the process. Yes, we are both Mossad agents."

"I appreciate your candor. For two Mossad agents to contact the San Francisco FBI field office, it must mean that you have a specific goal in mind. Before we begin, would you both like a cup of coffee?" Both declined.

"Agent Lomax, we understand that the FBI is conducting an investigation into the death of Nola Hetman and her daughter, Anna, and you are now looking into the death of Franz Detwrick."

"I'm sorry, but I am not at liberty to discuss an active investigation."

Segal smiled and looked at Cohen. "We anticipated you would say that, but if you could please call this number, I am sure you will be told of our offer to collaborate with your agency." She handed him a card with a Washington D.C. number. It did not appear to

Lomax to be any of the FBI exchange phone numbers. He called Darcy to verify the number before he made the call. She called back after a few seconds and verified the number as belonging to the State Department in Washington D.C.

He examined the card and then placed a phone call to the number. "Agent Lomax, I was expecting your call. My name is Dillan Crosby, and I am with the State Department, which I expect you have already verified. At this moment, you must have two Mossad agents in your office, Ariel Segal and Levi Cohen. You are to provide the two Mossad agents with any form of assistance possible. You will see, after your discussion with them, that their information is extremely delicate, to say the least. If you need more clarification regarding your cooperation with them, please, give me a call." He hung up, not waiting for a reply.

Lomax looked at Segal and Cohen. "Well, the US State Department said to give you all the cooperation this office can provide, so I guess it would be best to find out why you are here."

Jeannie's receptionist motioned for her and Ismail to meet her in the coffee room. "There are two representatives from the Israeli government with the SAC. He told me to have you both go to his office as soon as I saw you."

"Israeli? Do you know what it's about?" Jeannie asked.

"No, but Lomax did not seem very upset about meeting with them."

"Okay, let's go see what's happening," Jeannie said to Ismail. Coffee would have to wait.

"Agent Loomis, Agent Flores. These are Mossad agents, Segal and Cohen. Everyone shook hands. "I think you will be very interested in what they have to share about your double homicide. Maybe the briefing room would be better, then everyone can get a coffee or tea."

The conversation as they moved from the breakroom to the briefing room was dominated by Lomax talking about his visit to Tel Aviv a few years ago and how much he wanted to return and visit the ancient Masada fortress in a southern district of Israel, situated on top of an isolated mountain plateau.

"What's Masada?" Ismail asked.

Cohen answered his question. "Masada is one of our country's most popular tourist attractions and a national treasure. Around 66 A.D., a group of rebels, Jews, took refuge on the mountain top from pursuing Romans, hoping to crush their resistance to their rule. According to legend, a Roman legion later surrounded Masada and built a wall around the mountain and then, eventually, a siege ramp against the western face of the plateau. The ramp was completed in the spring of 73 A.D. After around two to three months of siege, the Romans finally breached the wall of the fortress with a battering ram."

"Upon entering, the Romans discovered that its defenders had chosen mass suicide and killing each other rather than give in to the Romans, and they had set all the buildings except the food storerooms ablaze. Nine hundred and sixty men, women, and children in total. Your Hollywood produced a very good film about it."

"Yes, I saw that movie, and because of that, I would really like to visit the site," Lomax replied.

"If you go, you have two choices to reach the top of the mountain. I would suggest you take the tram and not the goat trail. It is very challenging. Our newly graduated Israeli soldiers swear, "Masada shall not fall again" and make nighttime pilgrimages to the site as part of their initiation into the military."

The two Mossad agents sat across from Lomax, Jeannie, and Ismail. "Agents Segal and Cohen are aware of our double homicide. They met with me early this morning before you two arrived. Instead of me paraphrasing what they said, perhaps it would be better, if you don't mind, to start from the beginning since it is Jeannie and her team that you will be working with."

Jeannie glanced at Lomax, attempting to show her confusion about working with agents of a foreign government. He apparently did not notice.

Segal began the conversation. "Through our earlier discussion with Agent Lomax, he has confirmed that your agency is working on the murders of Nola Hetman and her daughter, Anna. They were tortured and killed for not revealing the whereabouts of a secret map and diary."

"A map and diary? Must contain some valuable information to die for," Ismail said in reply.

"Yes. Let me explain with some background information. By the way, Agent Lomax has an excellent knowledge of the time in history which I am about to refer to."

13

CHAPTER

"As you are aware, Lt. Franz Detwrick was an officer of the Waffen SS. His career really took off after his assignment to the Sobibor death camp around June 1942. Sobibor was a pure extermination camp. When transport trains arrived, only a select few were chosen for manual labor while the rest were quickly dispatched to the changing rooms, gas chambers, and crematoriums."

"In 1941, before Sobibor was fully operational, the Nazis had a very impressive network of railroads operating not just in Germany but also in their other occupied countries. Most of Europe was controlled by Hitler. Auschwitz and Dachau served as training centers for SS officers who would later be assigned to other concentration and death camps. We believe that Detwrick received his training at both camps while Sobibor was being constructed. I am sorry, there is so much to cover. Back to the railroads."

"Prior to 1941, Hitler used his vast railroad systems to transport troops and supplies initially to the western front, but after invading Russia, to the eastern front. However, in 1941, Hitler began using the trains increasingly to transport human cargo. Cargo destined for any number of death camps, but the majority going to Auschwitz, followed later by Treblinka, Belzec, and Sobibor." Segal turned to Cohen, who took over.

"In the fall of 1941, Nazi Germany implemented a plan to systematically murder the Jews. This plan was codenamed Operation Reinhold, the answer to their so-called Jewish question. New railroad lines had to be constructed to run to the secret locations of the death camps, which were mostly in eastern Poland. Detwrick designed a new railroad line leading to and into Sobibor. He was recognized for his work by no less than Hermann Goering. His design changes at Sobibor, after examining the railroad systems, forced the Nazis to re-examine the railroad lines to their other camps. Eventually, Detwrick was transferred to Austria." Jeannie felt herself go tense on hearing the word Austria. *Relax, girl; the Austrian government is not after your ass anymore.*

"I thought he was captured where Hitler killed himself?" Ismail asked.

"I will get to that, but please, there is much more to tell," Cohen said. "As the Nazis invaded villages, towns, and cities, their main army, after eliminating any resistance, moved on. Hitler's killing squads, called Einsatzgruppen, followed. They were SS death squads who were responsible for rounding up Jews and other undesirables. Many Jews were killed on the spot and buried in mass graves. Others, however, were later transported in cattle cars to the extermination camps."

"By 1944, even as the war was turning against Nazi Germany, Hitler was manufacturing high-speed trains to expedite the transportation of Jews. Day and night, these trains rumbled across the countryside." Cohen took a pause, and Segal took over.

"Now, where does Detwrick fit into this World War II history lesson? Well, besides the transportation of human cargo destined for the death camps, Hermann Goering, under orders from Hitler, was confiscating, no, the correct term would be stealing, anything of value found in the homes and on the person of Jews."

"He appointed Reichmarschall Goering to supervise the largest theft of paintings, silverware, jewelry, money, and anything else of value as bounty for the Nazi regime. These items were placed on specially marked high-speed trains with massive locks on the boxcar doors, and each carriage was marked with a large swastika. Each car had a contingent of heavily armed SS soldiers."

"So, this is the rumored gold train?" Jeannie asked.

"Yes, but as you see, this operation was going on in all the countries occupied by the Nazis. There was no way that all these riches could be placed on just one train," Cohen jumped in.

"You mean there are more than one gold train out there?" Ismail asked.

Segal leaned forward on the table. "Goering instructed that some of the items gathered by the Nazis be placed in his home and Hitler's various residences for their enjoyment. Hitler envisioned his favorite architect, Albert Speer, building a Führermuseum in his hometown of Linz, Austria, believing that the Nazis would be victorious. This was when the war was going well for the Nazis.

But after invading Russia, the tide began to turn against Hitler and his Third Reich. No one knows for sure when he realized that he may not win the war, but, at some point, he instructed Goering to start hiding their spoils of war."

"And the spoils of war, assuming that Germany was going to lose, were to finance or start up a new Reich?" Jeannie asked.

"Correct," Cohen replied.

"You see, and I am sorry for repeating myself, but when German soldiers captured new territories, Goering's troops came in just before or during the time the death squads were active. They not only raided private homes of wealthy Jews and so-called enemies of the state but also looted museums and churches. Add to this the enormous volume of valuables seized from the victims at the death camps before and after their murders."

"You see, as the Jews arrived at the extermination camps, they were ordered to surrender any valuables they still had with them. Some still tried to hide valuables on their person. After their gassing, gold and silver tooth fillings were removed, and their body cavities searched. This property was eventually delivered to Goering. He was now faced with a logistical nightmare. Where was he going hide so much wealth with the Allies and Russia advancing on Germany?" Silence filled the room.

"Goering began running out of mines and caves in which to hide the valuables. He and Hitler felt that Germany would not be the best place to hide their ill-gotten treasures since the Allies and Russia would tear Germany apart looking for it after the war. They felt it would be better to store it temporarily in occupied countries, a less likely place for the Allies to search."

"What do you mean, temporarily?" Jeannie asked.

"As the war was coming to an end and Hitler's vision of a thousand-year Reich was all but a dream, he and Goering believed they should store their stolen riches in secure locations, so it would be available for the Fourth Reich, as you said earlier," Segal said. "May we take a bathroom break?" she asked.

Lomax had arranged for bagels, lox, and donuts to be delivered to the briefing room. As everyone returned, each helped themselves to refreshments. Seated again, Cohen started the next session off. "As I said, Goering primarily chose salt mines and caves in which to hide the stolen property, but the sheer necessity of finding other places safe from enemy bombs forced him to construct tunnels."

Lomax asked that if the loot was to be hidden in mines, caves, and tunnels in occupied countries, does that mean these gold trains are in Poland, Romania, and even Italy?"

"Let us say that the State of Israel believes there are numerous places still holding the property of Jews in many countries. But that question, sir, brings us full circle back to Franz Detwrick and your double murder."

Cohen handed the presentation back to Segal. "Our information is that Lt. Detwrick, having the favor of Goering, was asked to supervise the tunneling operation of at least one such site. He used forced labor to construct the tunnel and then arrange for the gold train to be secured inside."

"So, you believe Detwrick had maps noting the location of the tunnel, and that is why Hetman and her daughter were killed? And, if that is the case, do you know who the killers are?" Jeannie asked.

"You, agent Loomis, probably best understand the existence of the Fourth Reich's Organization. These modern-day Nazis still carry Hitler's dream of a new Germany rising out of the ashes of the former Third Reich. We (looking at Cohen) and our agency believe that, somehow, the Organization learned of the existence of these maps that would lead them to Hitler's lost gold trains. It is they who killed the Hetmans."

14

CHAPTER

THE BRIEFING MERGED into lunch, with Lomax once again arranging for sandwiches, chips, and sodas to be delivered. "Do you believe that Detwrick had maps and a diary?" Jeannie asked.

"We do not know, but it appears that the Organization believes so, to the point of killing your two victims," Segal responded. "You see, Hitler knew he was running out of time by 1945 and issued an order called the Nero Decree, ordering the destruction of German infrastructure to prevent its use by the Allied forces as they penetrated deep within Germany. Albert Speer was to make sure Hitler's orders were carried out."

"But Speer refused to do so," Lomax interjected.

"That is true, but what many do not know is that Hitler's Nero Decree was to extend to most of the property secured by Goering. All statues, paintings, and books, anything but gold and silver, were to be burned or otherwise destroyed. If the Nazis could not enjoy them, no one else should be allowed to."

"Jesus," Ismail exclaimed, later realizing he had said the Lord's name in front of two Mossad agents.

"Hitler countermanded his own order, but many of the fanatical SS destroyed various storage locations and put the torch to numerous masterpieces. You Americans have another excellent film showing such events, called *The Monument Men*.

Knowing the SS were destroying valuable pieces of art, and with the destruction of Nazi Germany imminent to everyone's realization except Hitler's, Goering began storing some of the art in the Führerbunker in Berlin. He learned that Hitler would be conducting the defense of Germany from that location and felt that being surrounded by masterpieces might be good for his morale."

"Gee. The Allies were approaching from the west, and the Russians were heading towards Berlin from the east, yet Goering felt that Hitler might relax at times by admiring his stolen art. Got to love it," Ismail said. Only Cohen and Segal did not laugh.

"Not only that, but Hitler demanded increasing numbers of trains to divert from the fronts to transport more Jews to the death camps. We don't know why Detwrick was near the Führerbunker nor if he was arrested there for sure. We have mixed reports of the incident. But we do know that he was instructed by Goering to create a least one such tunnel."

"Detwrick did stand before the war crimes tribunal, but there was no direct evidence that could be found that would have led to his death sentence and hanging. Those that could have provided the evidence leading to his execution had already been killed. We hope that this information we have shared might help in your investigation. Sorry for taking so much of your time."

No one spoke for several seconds.

"It seems to me that the key to solving our double homicide hinges on what the killers are after and, if you are correct, we need to know the whereabouts of the maps and diary," Lomax said to no one in particular. "And with that in mind, I will let you fine agents get to it." He grabbed another soda and sandwich and left the briefing room.

Jeannie called for a break and began heading to the women's bathroom, noticing that several of her agents were gathered around her secretary's desk. She had forgotten she had ordered them there to get their assignments regarding the Hetman case. *Shit,* she said to herself. "Go to the briefing room. There might be some sandwiches, chips, and sodas left," she said as she approached them. "I will fill you in when I get back there."

With the addition of the other agents under Jeannie's command, the group had to reassemble in the larger briefing room. Once everyone took a seat, Jeannie addressed the group. "First, I apologize for you having to gather in the hallways. Frankly, I must admit that I forgot about the morning briefing I wanted you to attend. Guess I am getting old."

"The other reason for my lapse in memory is that early this morning, we met Agents Segal and Cohen from Israel." She pointed to the two agents. "They are here to assist us in our investigation and have provided us with a wealth of background information which I believe will help us solve this case."

Many agents tried to get a look at the two agents from Israel. Jeannie approached the large portable whiteboard and picked up a dry erase marker.

"Alright. This is what we know so far." She wrote on the board:

- Nola Hetman - fifty-four years old - Federal Court Interpreter with the Administrative Office of the US Courts. Only heir to estate of Detwrick.

"Steve, I want you and Angie to focus on interviewing her co-workers. Ismail and I have already talked with her supervisor and explored the possibility of a connection with her most recent case and came up with nothing. Examine her prior cases. See if that leads anywhere."

- Anna Hetman – seventeen years old. Daughter of Nola. High school student.

"Sam, go back to the school. Check her locker, including if she had one for PE. Contact her teachers, friends, any enemies. Anything you can find."

- Franz Detwrick – 101 years old – deceased. Uncle to Nola – SS Lt. Sobibor death camp and others?

"I need to give this one some thought after all the information Agents Segal and Cohen gave us. Let me sleep on it, and perhaps Ismail and I can focus on him." Cohen and Segal nodded in agreement.

"Darcy, you and Burk check on the finances of Detwrick and Hetman. Check for everything. This might give us some clues as to where to focus our investigation.

"Tony, you and Annette search phone records for all of them. Also, search any social media sites they might have used. Oh, and check on the history of Detwrick's computer usage. If you run into problems with passwords, etc., contact either Darcy or Burk."

"Ismail. See what the progress is on Hetman's car. Check with the SFO. Maybe it was

dumped in long-term parking. I can't believe it has not turned up yet. Also, get a search warrant in case Hetman or Detwrick had safe deposit boxes. Wait, we need to find out what bank Detwrick used. Go ahead and contact his neighbors. Maybe they helped him with getting his groceries, doctor's visits, etc. See what they know. Okay, people, I am sure I will have more things for us to do, but this will keep you busy for now."

The group took her final comments as being dismissed, so they filed out, leaving Cohen, Segal, and Ismail in the room. "Agent Loomis, I was impressed with your list of action items," Segal said. "Might we know if anything of interest was found inside either the Hetman's home or Detwrick's?"

"Sure. I will have my secretary run copies of the reports from our forensic team searches. Follow me. By the way, call me Jeannie." Jeannie's day ended with the long stop-and-go commute from San Francisco to Newark. *Mossad working with us. That's a first for me. I still feel I am missing something. What the hell is it? Another itch that I can't reach.*

15

CHAPTER

NO SOONER HAD Jeannie entered her home than her cell went off. "What do you think about our two Mossad agents?" Lomax asked before she could say hi.

"I think they know more than they are sharing if that's what you mean?"

"Exactly, yet I can't figure out their angle. I'm looking at this from the point of view that if there is a map and/ or diary and it leads to an actual gold train, then what?"

"That crossed my mind as well, along with how much they know about the Organization. Let's say an actual gold train is located. Who takes possession?" Jeannie asked.

"If a train is found, whether this one or one in any number of other hiding places Goering used, I am sure the case will be tied up in litigation for years. Let's cooperate with them, but at the same time, certain things might need to stay in-house, if you get my drift?"

***

As soon as Segal and Cohen got back to their hotel, Cohen called Tel Aviv. "What did you learn from our friends, the Americans?" the male voice asked upon answering.

"We are both sure they know more than they are sharing, and that was assumed. Their chief investigator, an Agent Jeannie Loomis, appears to be a well-organized and aggressive investigator, so working with them should be a great asset. Today, we met with her supervisor Lomax and her team and provided a limited background report on Detwrick. She instructed her agents in what avenues needed to be explored."

"When will you two be allowed to search Detwick's residence?

"We did not want to push them in that direction yet, since we are sure they do not totally trust us, but they provided reports of what they found during their initial search of his residence, which I will send to you after this call."

"Okay, keep me appraised."

***

At two o'clock in the morning, Jeannie was awakened by the vibration of her phone. *Nothing good comes from a phone call at 2 a.m.* "Loomis," she said after clearing her throat.

"Agent Loomis, this is Sergeant Ballard, SFPD. We just chased off a person trying to break into that house you have sealed off on Grant Street. Some neighbors saw two white males standing outside the house on the sidewalk. One of them walked up to the front door, and it looks like, from the teeth marks we found on the door handle, they tried to use channel locks to open it. A Chinese gentleman asked them what they were doing. They got scared and ran down the street. By the time we got there, they were long gone. Thought you would want to know, so I called the cell number you gave me."

Jeannie got off the phone and called Ismail. "Hey, you know what time it is, boss lady? A guy like me needs my beauty sleep."

"Are you through? Yes, I know what time it is. SFPD just called. Someone tried to break into Detwrick's home this morning."

"You think it might be our Mossad friends?" Ismail asked.

"The thought crossed my mind. SFPD will watch the house until daybreak. Go back to sleep, and I will meet you at the house at nine if that gives you enough beauty sleep?"

At 9 a.m., Jeannie saw Ismail's pickup parked in front of the residence on Grand Street. "Good morning, Ace," Jeannie said, handing him a Dutch Brothers coffee and a bag with two donuts. What do we have?"

"Hey, thanks for breakfast. SFPD was right. The perps tried to use a pair of channel locks on the door. One thing about these old homes is they're built tough, not like the new construction going on today. They could have broken the glass, but that would have brought too much attention. When I got here, a uniformed officer gave me the name of the reporting party who chased them away. Want to go talk to him?"

Min Yang was a forty-one-year-old male who lived next door to Detwrick. He was smoking a cigarette when Jeannie and Ismail contacted him. His fingertips had yellow nicotine stains. He told Jeannie and Ismail that he had just gotten home from his job as a cook at one of Chinatown's exclusive restaurants. He saw two white males, dressed in dark pants and jackets, standing in front of the residence. They did not see Yang, who was seated in his car checking his text messages and having a final smoke. When he saw one of the males walk up to the door, he knew something was up since he was aware that Detwrick had died. He asked them what they were doing, and they quickly took off.

Due to the darkness and poor street lighting, he doubted he could provide any detailed information that could be developed into a sketch. The only good information they gleaned from Yang's interview was the name of the neighbor who helped Detwrick with his groceries and doctor's appointments. Unfortunately, that neighbor had left for China two days before, and Yang did not know when she would be returning. He would check to see if he had her cell phone number.

They walked together back to their respective cars. "Well, at least Segal wasn't one of the two, but that doesn't mean she wasn't in the area," Ismail said.

"True, but why establish a working relationship with us and then do a dumb thing like that? Doesn't add up. I think there are some other characters involved, but who? Possibly the suspects that killed the Hetmans?"

"You mean the Organization?"

"Yup."

16

CHAPTER

SEGAL AND COHEN were waiting in the breakroom talking about Masada with Lomax. "Good morning," Jeannie said as she and Ismail got their first cups of coffee for the day. After she doctored up her coffee, she turned and looked directly at the two Mossad agents. "The reason we are late is that someone tried to break into Detwrick's house early this morning."

"Did they gain entrance?" Lomax asked. Jeannie said no and did not notice anything suspicious in the faces or body language of either Cohen or Segal. *Doesn't mean they weren't involved. They are trained to lie, just like us, when the situation calls for it.*

"No. A neighbor coming home from work scared them off. They were trying to force the front door lock with a pair of channel locks pliers," Ismail added. "He didn't get a good look at them. Two white males in their forties. Dark clothing. No vehicle seen."

"Huh," Lomax said as he left the three agents in the breakroom.

"Obviously, whoever they were, they believe something valuable is still in the house," Cohen said. "We reviewed your search team's reports, and it appears that they were quite thorough." He left his comments hanging in the air, hoping that Jeannie or Ismail would address them, but neither did.

Jeannie said, "I kept going over the details you two laid out yesterday about Detwrick's background and his Nazi past with the SS. I understand that your agency feels that perhaps he was placed in a position by Goering to supervise the movement and storage of that particular gold train, and I tend to come to the same conclusion. But my boss and I still wonder why he was captured near the Führerbunker. If the war was coming to an end, why didn't he try to escape with the rest of the rats?"

Segal took a sip of her coffee and glanced at Cohen. "Our agency has a lot of knowledge about the final days of Hitler that we received from the interrogations of former Nazis." Jeannie and Ismail wondered what type of interrogation techniques Mossad used.

"As the war was coming to an end, many Nazis who held certain high levels in the party saw the opportunity to flee and have a future. We know that many of the SS had stolen property that they never turned over to the Reich. Jewelry, money, gold, diamonds, paintings, you name it."

"Detwrick, if he did have knowledge of the wealth contained on this gold train, could have skimmed some for his personal use. Sure, if an SS officer was caught with Nazi confiscated goods, he would have been shot on the spot or, earlier in the war, transferred to the Russian front. We believe that Detwrick did steal from the train, adding to the valuables he took from the victims at the death camps, yet he kept up the appearance of being a trusted SS officer. We feel he went to see Hitler personally to assure him the gold train was secure and perhaps give him maps leading to its location."

Jeannie quickly processed this information. "So, you think that he gave a copy of the map to Hitler but had a duplicate map for himself to use after the war?"

"Correct, as well as possibly a personal diary," Cohen said. "And we believe that since you did not find it in his house, nor did the Hetmens' killers; he must have it in a safe deposit box somewhere."

"I tend to agree with your assessment, but there are numerous banks, not to mention credit unions, in San Francisco. We will try to contact all of them, but it is not an easy task. I thought of another thing last night. I'm wondering if Detwrick still has living friends from the war years and if they are still alive. How many others were fortunate to live to be 101 years old like him? To check that out will also take a tremendous amount of time and involve law enforcement agencies in various countries."

There seemed to be some hesitation between the two Mossad agents. Finally, Cohen spoke up. "Agent

Loomis, suffice to say that our agency has exhausted the discovery of any of Detwrick's living friends or family members, except for the late Hetman's. We are certain that all of his known associates in the SS are dead."

"You sound very certain," Ismail said.

"Detwrick had one close SS associate, a Sergeant Otto Meyer, who died ten weeks ago in Austria. At one time, the two worked at the Ohrdruf concentration camp. This was a subcamp of the Buchenwald and the first Nazi camp liberated by your American troops. By the time we located Meyer, he was on his death bed, but he did admit that he knew Detwrick and that Detwrick had bragged one night while intoxicated that he knew the location of Hitler's gold train. He swore until he died that he had no other information."

Jeannie thought to herself that she and Lomax were correct. These two were holding back information. "So, now we have confirmation that Detwrick at least bragged that he knew the location of Hitler's phantom gold train. No mention of a map or diary?"

"None, and like I said, when our agents located him, he was near death. He also had no surviving friends or family, so there were no more leads to follow."

"I do not know how familiar you are with our laws here in the United States, but for us to access bank records, we must secure a search warrant for each and every financial institution. Darcy, my go-to technology expert, and her partner are handling that as we speak, but it will take time."

"We understand. There is something else you need to know." Segal said almost in a whisper. "Our agency is aware that the Nazis are also searching for Detwrick's map. Members of their Organization were probably the ones responsible for trying to break into his house this morning."

"I'm glad you feel you can trust us by bringing up this matter. When I first met the two of you in Lomax's office, you mentioned that I was aware of the Organization. That is true. Working with Interpol, we were searching for a Doctor Hausser, an SS officer within their Organization. During our investigation, he was killed, and I was wounded." The look on the two Mossad officers told Jeannie they already had that knowledge. "So, you believe they are actively following the same leads we have?"

"Yes. The network, or as they call themselves, the Organization, is international, and they have penetrated corporations, businesses, and even governments." Jeannie thought of her recent suspension due to the Austrian government's accusation of her committing a murder in their country. The Organization pushed for reprisal for the killing of Dr. Hausser and her extradition, but it was coming from heat brought on by the Organization.

"Our government believes that their intelligence network is greater than ours, thus our reaching out to you. We should have been upfront with you and agent Lomax. We do apologize," Cohen said.

17

CHAPTER

JEANNIE HAD ONE of her agents give Segal and Cohen a tour of the bureau while she met with Lomax. "They are offering bits and pieces, but I don't think they are withholding anything earth-shattering," Jeannie said.

"Good to know. Any progress?"

"Not yet, just a bunch of background information, although they did tell me that Detwrick had a war buddy, Otto Meyer, who he'd worked with at Ohrdruf concentration camp, who confirmed on his recent death bed that Detwrick had bragged when drunk that he knew the whereabouts of Hitler's phantom train." Lomax indicated that he knew about the Ohrdruf camp.

"Still, could be bullshit," Lomax said. "What's your next move?"

"Would it be possible for you to use your 'contacts' and find anything you can about this Sergeant Otto Meyer? It appears Mossad quickly dismissed him, staying focused instead on Detwrick. I want to make sure there is nothing else there. He was also old when he died, so there are probably no living relatives, but who knows. Maybe your contacts can find associates, neighbors, doctors, nurses, anyone that he may have told stories to about Detwrick and the gold train."

"I like that avenue of inquiry. I still have some old buddies in Europe that owe me some favors. Maybe Mossad missed something in his war trial since I assume he faced war crimes if he was in the Waffen SS and assigned to Ohrdruf concentration camp."

"I'm having Darcy and Burk hit the banks real hard. In an ideal world, we'll find a safe deposit box that will reveal everything." She laughed.

"Stranger things have happened, that's for damn sure," Lomax said before answering his ringing phone. Jeannie waved goodbye and checked in with her secretary.

There, she found a call from a Susan Chin in the middle of a stack of While-You-Were-Out notices. *Where had she heard that name before?* "Hey, boss, they found Hetman's car, but before you get too excited, whoever took it burnt it to a shell. Forensics was sent out but could not find anything useful. It was in an unincorporated area in San Mateo. No cameras in the area. Guess we can cross that off the list."

Jeannie heard what Ismail was saying but was still trying to determine why the name Susan Chin meant something. "Do you know a Susan Chin?" she asked.

"Yeah, that's the neighbor who used to take care of Detwrick. Remember, she wasn't home when we talked to the guy who chased away the burglar. She was in China and probably still is. He must have found her cell phone number and called her. Why?"

"Shit, that's where I heard the name." She showed him the note with the phone number. "Hey, now that I solved the case of the missing Hetman car, you want me to call her and do my normal expert interview?"

Jeannie smiled, rolled her eyes, and said, "Please do, kind sir."

"Flattery will get you everywhere."

Jeannie returned to her office, where she made her way through the other phone messages. Finding nothing urgent, she closed her door and sat in her chair. She tilted the chair back as far as it would go and closed her eyes. She could tell a headache was coming. She didn't know how much time had passed when she heard a knock on the door.

"Come in. It's open," she said, after sitting up and making it look like she was returning phone calls.

"Hey, I think I got something," an excited Ismail said while holding a piece of paper in his hand. "Chin said that she had been taking care of Detwrick for almost eight years. He was always nice to her, but she found him a little scary. She hated his display of Nazi medals hanging on the wall. She said he was very proud of them and wasn't repentant or ashamed."

"Once a week, she would go grocery shopping for him and occasionally drove him to his doctor. He rarely carried on a conversation, usually just saying what his doctor had told him. She described him as a loner, which was not surprising since he had outlived all his friends. By the way, I have the doctor's name, also due to my expert interviewing skills." Jeannie did not bite and waited for him to return to the matter at hand.

"Okay. I asked her how he paid her for groceries. She said he always had a lot of cash on hand and insisted on giving her a large tip for her trouble. One time, when his arthritis had really flared up, he dropped his money as he was trying to retrieve it from his sweater pocket. She helped him pick up the cash and saw a large wad of $100 bills, at least a thousand bucks. She told me he banks at that Wells Fargo bank in Stockton. I gave the info to Burk and Darcy, and they are securing a search warrant from legal."

"Great job, Ace. Might be the break we need. Let's go and tell Lomax and our friends from Israel."

With a search warrant in hand, Ismail, Jeannie, Cohen, and Segal entered the banking branch used by Detwrick. After identifying themselves, the bank manager secured the documents they requested but stated that Detwrick never had a safe deposit box with them. A quick pursual by Jeannie of the banking documents which she shared with everyone showed a monthly balance of always around $10,000. More interesting was that every other month, another $9,999 was deposited, always in cash.

"What does this tell you?" Cohen asked.

"Well, it could mean that old Detwrick knew that if he deposited $10,000 or more in cash too many times, our Internal Revenue Service, our federal tax agency, might come knocking on his door."

Ismail could tell from their faces that they were confused. "You see, to try to track down drug dealers and terrorists, our banks, credit unions, and other financial institutions are required by law to notify them if extremely large or continuing deposits over $10,000 in cash are made. Sets off an alarm, so to speak."

"Hmm. Or it could mean that Lt. Detwrick did not want to bring attention to himself," Segal added. "So, once again, we are back to square one."

"Maybe not. You two will be amazed at the ability our two techno wizards have to turn stuff up," Jeannie said as the four were leaving the bank. "Let's go back to the office and see what the rest of the team has found."

Lomax was waiting for them when they arrived. "Judging from your faces, no luck."

Jeannie filled him in about the bank documents and that she would have Darcy and Burk continue to dig, especially on where the deposits originated from. She also told him about what Ismail had learned from the neighbor. "Sounds like you still need something to break the case."

Berlin

Heiliger was pacing in his office. It had been almost four days, and they were no closer to securing the maps and diary from Detwrick's house. The rumors were growing about his inability to lead the Organization and the possibility of forcing him out of his leadership role or simply eliminating him. He picked up his phone and placed the call.

Klaus Rictner answered on its first ring. "Yes, sir."

"What is the status of getting into Detwrick's house? Members of the Organization are growing restless. What is it taking so long?"

"Sir, we attempted to enter the home early this morning, but before we could get in, a neighbor saw us and called the police."

"Police? Do they know about us? This could be a disaster!"

"No, sir. We got away, and no one followed. We are now continuing to watch the house."

18

CHAPTER

A WEEK PASSED, and still not much progress. On Wednesday morning, Lomax knocked on Jeannie's door, holding several pieces of paper. "Let's get some coffee," he said as he headed down the hallway. While walking, he told Jeannie that he got a lot of information from his friends regarding Detwrick's SS buddy Sergeant Otto Meyer.

After getting their coffees, they sat at the table. Lomax laid out the papers he had been carrying. "Ohrdruf camp did not come into existence until late in the war. It was created in November 1944 near the city of Gotha, Germany. I visited the city with my wife several years ago, and it is quite pretty. Anyway, initially, it was an independent site under the SS Main Economic and Administrative Office, and eventually, it became a sub-camp of Buchenwald.

Ohrdruf supplied forced labor in the form of concentration camp prisoners for, get this, railway construction leading to a proposed communications center. However, due to the rapid advance of US forces, the communication center was never completed."

"In late March 1945, the camp had a prisoner population of over 10,000. In early April, the SS evacuated almost all the prisoners on death marches to Buchenwald. The SS guards killed many of the remaining prisoners who were too sick to walk to the railcars.

The Third US Army liberated Ohrdruf on April 4, 1945, so Detwrick, if he had been assigned there, had already been reassigned. Now, back to SS Sgt. Meyer and something that I found very, very interesting."

"As I think I said, the camp supplied forced labor in the form of concentration camp prisoners for a planned railway construction project for an immense communications center inside the basement of the Muhlberg Castle in Ohrdruf. Here's a picture of the castle."

Inmates had to work to connect the castle to the main railroad line and to dig tunnels into the nearby mountains, which would be used as an emergency shelter for a train." Jeannie's eyes were the size of saucers.

"Jesus. Sounds like a job for old Detwrick, huh? Relocate railroad tracks and dig tunnels. Right up his alley," Jeannie said while studying the photo.

"It gets better," Lomax said. "My friends found records from the camp that showed that, in fact, Detwrick supervised Sgt. Meyer while at Ohrdruf and later arranged for his transfer to work with him in Litz, Austria."

"There's the connection. Gee, our Mossad friends didn't tell us this detail, did they?" Jeannie asked.

"No, they did not. This Sgt. Meyer was a brutal bastard. At the end of the war, he was caught wearing a private's uniform, but the way some of the other German POWs acted around him caused the Americans to conduct a complete body search, and they found his blood type tattooed in his armpit."

"Oops, that's a got ya!" Jeannie said with a smile on her face.

"Meyer initially supervised the camp's slave labor. He instituted workdays that began with ten- to eleven-hour-long shifts, but later, he increased these to fourteen hours, and it involved strenuous physical labor building roads, railways, and tunnels.

In addition, inmates had to cope with long marches and musterings, a total lack of sanitary equipment or medical facilities, and insufficient food and clothing. There was a saying in Ohrdruf when Sgt. Meyer was present, "You fall, you die."

During his war crimes trial, several former inmates testified that they witnessed him kill up to twenty people a day just for fun, but his defense attorney stated it was all hearsay, so that is probably why he got thirty years like Detwrick, instead of the rope."

"The Allies had a pretty tight case of war crimes against the sergeant who got a thirty-year sentence in Spandau Prison where our Detwrick was also serving time.

"There is another record showing Meyer being transferred to a unit that Detwrick supervised dealing with the re-routing of railroad tracks, but with the Americans approaching, he left the camp with no indication as to his destination."

"I bet Detwrick recognized his ability regarding the re-routing of track or his ability to create tunnels, and with his new directive from Goering about the phantom train, Detwrick arranged for his transfer. Makes perfect sense," Jeannie said.

"I agree," Lomax responded, getting himself a second cup of coffee. "Meyer hung out with two people in Spandau during exercise periods besides Detwrick. One hanged himself in his cell in less than three months, but the other became a close friend.

His name was Ludwig Speer; no relationship to Albert Speer, Hitler's architect."

"Ludwig wrote letters to his wife during his time in prison. Most were about how life was inside Spandau, but he also mentioned that he knew the location of one of the Führer's gold trains, and once he got out, he promised they would be rich. This information must have come from Meyer."

"The plot thickens," is all Jeannie could think of saying.

"At Ludwig Speer's war crime trial, his counselor tried to bargain for a lighter sentence, offering to give up the location of Hitler's gold train." Jeannie leaned forward in her chair. "The next morning, Ludwig was found dead in his cell with the remains of a cyanide capsule in his mouth."

"Think it was Detwrick or Meyer's work to keep the secret quiet?" Jeannie asked. Lomax just raised both his hands and displayed a smile.

"I don't think Meyer ever knew exactly where the gold train ended up since Detwrick once again arranged for his transfer, this time to return and defend Berlin. There must have been a falling out between the two. Whatever Meyer confiscated for himself from Jewish prisoners has never been found. His wife recently died, and before her death, she lived modestly."

"Maybe Detwrick planted some loot in Meyer's possession and threatened to turn him in to the Gestapo.

Meyer pleaded for his life, and an arrangement for his transfer to Berlin settled the matter," Jeannie offered.

"Works for me, but we will never know. Let's keep this new information to ourselves. But now we know that our friends from Israel are not giving us all their information."

19

CHAPTER

JEANNIE ORDERED EVERYONE in for a briefing slated for noon. She arranged for pizza, salad, and drinks to be delivered. Everyone still seemed to be in a relatively good mood, with no signs of frustration setting in yet. She listed each team on the board in the order she wanted them to report regarding their progress and findings. Darcy and Burk were first up.

"Detwrick kept a balance in his saving and checking account combined, never exceeding $10,000. But, with the deposits in the form of cash, with $9,999 coming in on the first of each month, there is nothing to track. The bank verified that he arrived around the first of each month. Tellers remember him due to his age and always having the money in a brown paper bag. Sometimes he took a withdrawal. Obviously, there is something there. We need more time," Burk said, turning the floor over to Darcy.

"By the way, these deposits have been occurring ever since his release from Spandau Prison after his relocation to the US," she said before proceeding. "We have confirmed that his house is paid for. He paid cash when he first bought the residence with his wife. Neither she nor Detwrick had any insurance policies that we have found. Those banks that would cooperate with us without a search warrant all indicated the lack of a safe deposit box. If he kept any records of his financial dealings, we have not found them yet."

"A review of his computer usage shows that he liked to play video games. It does not appear that he was into gambling, at least not on the Internet. He primarily watched movies on YouTube, and only occasionally did he stream a newly released video."

Jeannie's other agents did their report-outs. When everyone had finished presenting their progress, they all came to the same conclusion. They needed to find physical documentation, whether it be a map, diary, or journal, before they could proceed. Jeannie sent everyone home after a long day. Segal and Cohen told Jeannie they were impressed with the work her team had shared and tried to reassure her that her team was getting close to a big break.

Jeannie walked with Ismail to the secured parking lot. "Looks like another dead end," Ismail said.

"I agree. This Detwrick asshole was good at covering his tracks. I had my hopes of finding a safe deposit box that would bring everything full circle and wrap up the investigation, but as Segal so eloquently said, "We are back at square one."

Surprisingly, sometimes being stranded in your car during a commute smelling exhaust fumes can stimulate your mind or put you to sleep. The proverbial light bulb came on mid-span on the Dumbarton Bridge. Jeannie remembered that when she and Ismail had checked out Detwrick's house while the forensic team was present, she had a very strange feeling, but she could not put her finger on it. They needed to do another search of both residences, Detwrick's and the Hetmen's.

She had a restless night trying to rationalize why she felt she had missed something inside the house on Grant. *What could the forensic team have missed?* Her thoughts wandered back to her search of her cabin in Idaho after forensics had concluded their search, hoping that she might find some elusive clue about Frank Silva and the Banshees, but came up empty. She had hoped that Silva may have hidden information on the location of the Ark of the Covenant and his plans after stealing it. *God, let us find something in those houses tomorrow.*

The next day, on her way to the bureau, Jeannie called both Ismail and the SAC, telling them about her plan to re-search Detwrick's residence as well as Nola's. "I assume you will be inviting our two 'agent guests?'" Lomax asked.

"That's the plan, but Ismail and I will be at their sides monitoring their movements."

"I made a few phone calls to people owing me a favor or two regarding Cohen and Segal. Not only are they Mossad, which they have already told us, but they are an assassin team that has been very successful in locating hidden Nazis and their sympathizers. Of course, as time marches on, most of those WWII Nazis who were able to hide have died, like Detwrick. My sources tell me that if they are no longer hunting Nazis and have focused on the mythical 'Phantom Train,' then they must have some good intel."

"My sources also said that it is highly unlikely that they are here alone. In other words, Mossad is probably not only watching them but us too. It's your investigation but consider whether you want me to put surveillance on them for security."

"I was thinking about that and another thing on my drive in this morning. If you recall, when those two males tried to burglarize the Detwrick's house the other morning and got scared off, they vanished very quickly. I think they had a standby car, probably with at least a driver, helping them escape. Perhaps Segal was the driver, which means that there is still at least one additional Mossad agent with them. Go ahead and put surveillance on them, but they need to be the best we have. These guys have been trained to spot them."

20

CHAPTER

AFTER ARRIVING AT the bureau and checking in with her secretary and team members, Jeannie met with Ismail, Segal, and Cohen. "I've decided that we need to re-search both houses, starting with the Hetman's house in Half Moon Bay. I know forensics did an excellent job, but something has to be in one of those two homes that will give us a lead or two."

"Would it be expeditious if you and Agent Flores searched Hetman's home and Levi and I searched Detwrick's?" Segal asked. Jeannie noted that Segal offered that the two of them search the Grand Street house. *They believe something is there.*

"I would much rather we four search each house using a grid method. Ismail and I will show you when we get there. Let's meet back here in ten to fifteen minutes, getting bathroom and coffee breaks out of the way." Ismail followed Jeannie down the hall to the restroom leaving the two Mossad agents alone in the breakroom.

"What grid method in searching a house are you talking about?" Ismail asked, knowing that Jeannie just threw the term out there, hoping to not only confuse the Mossad agents but also to justify why she wanted them with her and Ismail.

"The SAC told me that they are both part of an exceptional hit team for Mossad. They are normally Nazi hunters, but apparently, their agency really believes that the phantom gold train exists. Neither Lomax nor I have figured out their end game, but we need to watch them like hawks. Also, think about this. Lomax's sources said that it is very rare for only two Mossad agents to be working together. In other words, they normally work in teams of three or more. So, with that in mind, think about the attempted burglary the other morning."

"Understood. Cohen and another male agent attempted the break-in while old Ariel Segal sat in the getaway car. I can see that."

The drive to Half-Moon-Bay was uneventful. The conversation in the car, driven by Ismail, varied from the weather in the bay area compared to Israel, Alcatraz Island, politics, and things they did while growing up.

They reached the Hetman's residence. Ismail removed the tape, and the four entered. The house had a stale smell as if vacant for longer than it had been. "Here is how we conduct a grid search," Jeannie said. Ismail, whose back was to them, just smiled to himself. Ariel and I will search the kitchen and dining room. You start on one side of the room and I on the other. We will meet here (pointing to a position in the room). Then we switch sides and re-search where the other person has been. I know it sounds a little rudimentary, but it is highly effective."

Ismail and Cohen took the master bedroom and Anna's room. They finished before Jeannie and Segal, so they took on the third bedroom and bathrooms. They met up with Jeannie and Segal in the kitchen. The search had been completed and yielded nothing to further their investigation. During the search, Jeannie could sense that Segal had no interest in Hetman's residence. That would change once back in San Francisco at the SS officer's house.

It was past 1 p.m. by the time they got to Grand Street.

***

"You have something to report?" Rictner asked upon answering the call from Erwin Mueller.

"Yes, sir. The police are back. The two FBI agents from the other day and two other people, a man and a woman. They are not wearing any jackets with letters on them, so I do not know who they are with. What should we do?" There was a brief pause.

"I have a feeling they might be on to something. It is time for us to take action. More soldiers are on the way. Just keep observing and call me every five minutes with an update." Rictner hung up and placed a phone call to Gunter Schneider. "Get your teams in position, now!"

Ismail removed the crime scene tape and pushed open the front door to Detwrick's residence. All four entered and climbed the few stairs leading to the first floor. "This time, I want to do the search slightly differently. Ariel and I will search the first floor, and you and Ismail will start on the second. Once you have finished your search, come back down here, or we will come up to you, and we will each search the room the others just completed. Any questions?"

"What if each of us took a room, since there are four levels, and then rotate in a similar fashion?" Cohen asked.

"Not a bad idea, but this is an extremely old house. With Detwrick being a former SS officer, I want to make sure safety is our primary concern. So, let's get started. Ismail, Levi, second floor, and Ariel, you and I can start here." *An obvious attempt to be in a room alone, Jeannie thought.* Ismail had come to the same conclusion.

"You know, all the time we have been together, I don't think I have asked how long you and Levi have worked together?" Jeannie asked.

"Not very long," was the response. *Another lie,* Jeannie noted. "He and I worked for different departments before being assigned to this investigation. He was excited about coming to the United States for the first time. *Wonder if that's also a lie?*

The house was in shambles from first being trashed by the murderers, then disturbed by the search by the forensic team. The first floor had a kitchen, bathroom, and one bedroom. It looked like Detwrick was using this bedroom rather than any on the other floors. Segal really got into the search. She examined every book, every piece of furniture, cabinets, and coffee and sugar containers. In the bedroom, where the mattress had been thrown on the floor, she asked Jeannie for permission to tear it open. "Go for it," Jeannie said.

"Looks like Detwrick used this as his master bedroom instead of the top floor units. God, for someone receiving deposits of $10,000 a month, he certainly didn't spend it on housekeepers, new carpets, or drapes or anything," Segal said.

"I agree. What's amazing is that he does not appear to have been a hoarder. He didn't seem to collect anything. He cleaned up after himself. I don't see any raw garbage under the sink or in the bathroom, nor any cockroaches. It's like he prided himself on living a Spartan lifestyle. But what did he spend the $10,000 a month he was receiving on?" Jeannie asked.

Segal checked under each drawer for hidden items, including false compartments. She followed

Jeannie's action of tapping on the walls for hollow sounds. Nothing was left unexamined. Because of her attention to detail, Jeannie was able to watch Segal out of the corner of her eye, making sure nothing was found and hidden by the Mossad agent without being reported.

Ismail and Cohen found nothing on the second floor, which had a study, a spare bedroom, and a fairly large-sized bathroom. "You said, Agent Flores, that Mrs. Hetman was planning on selling this place?"

Ismail was a little surprised as when searching the Hetman's house, very few words had been spoken between them. "Yes, the real estate market in California, but especially in San Francisco, is crazy right now. This place, even in lousy shape, will easily sell for close to $2 million or more. That is if she had sold it "as-is," you know, without repairs. If, as her neighbor said, they were going to do a little cleaning and then have a painting crew come in, who knows how much money she would have made on its sale."

Finishing the first two stories and still coming up empty, Jeannie suggested that Cohen and she take the top floor while Ismail and Ariel did the third. "The way things are going, I don't know if it will be necessary to switch rooms after we are through. This may be another dead end."

"I agree," Segal said while looking at Cohen. Both looked defeated. "I think this staircase has seen better days," Jeannie said as she and Levi reached the top floor.

21

CHAPTER

"THEY HAVE BEEN in the house a long time. What do you think?" Hans asked Mueller. "How the fuck do I know? Just keep watching and shut up. The sound of Mueller's cell phone vibrating filled the van. Mueller looked at the phone and knew it would be Rictner again.

"Report," commanded Rictner.

"All four people are still in the house. They have not come outside since they entered.

I think that if they had found something, they would have already left the house or requested more officers to come."

The search was complete. All four were exhausted. "I could sure go for a hot shower and a thick steak and mashed potatoes," Ismail said. Jeannie laughed and looked at the faces of the two Mossad agents.

"My partner here is always hungry. I can't explain why he is not the size of an elephant."

"You must have a great metabolism, Agent Flores," Cohen said. Something was bugging Jeannie. Something felt off on the first floor. Ismail noticed a quizzical look on her face but didn't ask what was wrong. They made it to the front entryway when Jeannie stopped.

"What's wrong, boss?" Ismail asked. Jeannie did not answer. She was lost in thought. *What is it that's off?* she asked herself. Finally, she snapped out of it.

"Give me a second," she said as she climbed the stairs back to the top floor and entered the largest room. She moved to the center of the room and, while turning, looked at each wall. Then, using her feet to measure heel to toe, walked from corner to corner around the room. She noted the measurements. She did the same in the largest rooms on the third and second floors. The measurements were the same.

"What's up?" Ismail asked as she entered the first floor, with the two Mossad agents looking on. Jeannie did not answer. They all followed her into the room. The three watched as Jeannie, in the largest room next to the kitchen, again measured with the strides of her feet. The measurements were off. She looked at the three.

"There is a false wall here. A very solid wall that did not produce an echo when we tapped on it. See if we can find a hammer," Jeannie said.

"No, wait," an excited Ismail said. "Think about it. You are 101 years old. You are crippled with arthritis.

You created a hiding space in this room. You would not wall it in and not be able to access it, nor would you be swinging a hammer to gain entrance. Check everyone. There must be a hidden latch."

"Good job, Ace," Jeannie said.

Everyone began tapping on the wall and pushing on the crown molding. Nothing. Dejected, they stood in the center of the room. "Why would the measurements be off?" Jeannie asked. No one had an answer. She kicked the debris on the floor. "Damn it."

Something slid from under the garbage covering the rug. "What the hell is this?" she said while bending down. She realized it was a tuning fork. She pulled it out of the debris and raised it to the group, smiling.

She went to the wall and struck the tuning fork. Part of the wall opened like a door revealing a large hidden room. As the door opened, lights automatically turned on inside. Her heart began to race. Inside the room were numerous pictures of Detwrick dressed in his Waffen SS uniform watching Jews being led into the gas chamber.

"These are photos of different death camps, Segal said. This is Dachau, this one is Sobibor, and, of course, this one is Auschwitz. More medals hung on the wall. There were paintings, statues, and numerous coffee cans. An SS and swastika flag were mounted on the wall, and between them was a picture of Adolf Hitler.

"The guy sure liked coffee," Ismail said. Still wearing his plastic gloves, he removed the plastic cover from one of the cans. "Oh, Jesus," he said. "It's full of gold teeth fillings."

"Okay, stop, everyone. Don't touch anything. I'm going to call forensics and let them conduct a proper search. We don't want to screw up our case in our excitement. Ismail, take some photos with your phone showing the place as we found it. You two can do the same if you wish." While saying this, she and Ismail watched for reactions from the Mossad agents. If they were going to do something, now would be the opportune time. Instead, they followed Jeannie's orders.

***

"Sir, something is happening. Those officers who did the search the other day, the ones wearing hazmat clothing, are back. The police must have found something," an excited Mueller said as soon as Rictner answered his phone. "Now what?"

"Listen closely. While you have been watching the house, two teams of soldiers have taken up positions down the street from you on both sides. You two still have the best vantage point to see what is happening. Keep me on the phone. When it appears that they are taking items out of the house, immediately relay the information so our assault teams can move it. Do not engage. They will think you are police officers, and you will be shot. When the shooting is over, and it is safe, you and Hans can leave your post."

"What have you found?" asked Marsha as she and three other suited-up techs entered the first floor of the residence and focused on a door on the northern wall unnoticed during their search.

"A tone-activated wall. Pretty sophisticated. Ismail only touched this coffee can, but he was gloved up. Nothing else has been disturbed."

"Going to make yourself a fresh pot, Flores?" Marsha asked while laughing.

"It's full of human teeth," he said in reply.

"Get the fuck out of here. Are you for real?" she asked.

"Check for yourself," Ismail said. She opened the same can that Ismail had handled. "Jesus," she said. She instructed one of her techs to begin recording the new crime scene – a hidden room. Jeannie and the other three stood on the opposite side of the room and observed since it was too small for more than Marsha and maybe one of her techs to be in the secret room at one time.

"Eleven coffee cans of gold, each weighing approximately 10 pounds – looks like gold teeth fillings," Marsh said out loud as she made her way from one side of the room to the other. As she retrieved an item, she walked out of the room and placed it in a box. "This first box contains what might be diamonds. This one has rubies. My God, do you know how much this stuff is worth?" she asked, not expecting an answer.

Next, she came out of the room carrying a weapon. "This appears to be a Nazi semi-automatic with a Nazi swastika on it."

"Those were issued to SS officers," Cohen said.

Next came a vintage sub-machine gun. "This box contains ammo of various calibers. Let's see, one, two, three, looks like seventeen paintings. Holy shit, is this a Rembrandt?" Marsha asked.

She stopped searching, and everyone outside the hidden room admired the painting for a few minutes. "This son-of-a-bitch was hoarding things from old Adolf. There are more SS uniform shirts and pants, plus two pairs of highly polished boots on top of something. Let's put the clothing in these boxes." She returned to the room.

"Wow, I wonder how he got that badass safe up here? This is the largest antique Schwab safe I have ever seen." Give me a tape measure, will you, Bob?" After getting the tape, Marsha took the safe's measurements. "7 feet by 4 feet by 3 feet. This thing must weigh a ton. He had to have reinforced this floor to handle the weight." She invited Jeannie, Ismail, and the two Mossad agents to crowd together as best they could to get a look at the safe. "Do you have the combination?" she asked.

"No," Jeannie said. "But, let me try something. If he had to use the tuning fork to open the door, and with his age and degree of arthritis, why would he want to enter the combination each time? I mean, no one besides him knew it was here, right?" She put her plastic gloves back on and grabbed the handle of the safe and turned it. The safe opened.

The illumination from the lights the forensic team had set up, in addition to those installed by Detwrick, filled the room with gold, the light reflecting from 45 gold bars. Everyone gazed inside at its contents. "Oh, my God," Marsha said. She grabbed one of the bars and saw an inscription, *Reichsbank*. "This is Nazi gold." No one spoke.

Next to the gold bars were bundles of currency, with all but one having currency bands. "Looks like stacks and stacks of $10,000, with the exception of this one," Marsha said, pointing to a bunch of loose bills formerly in a stack like the others. "Guess he was working from this stack to pay the bills."

Jeannie's attention was on a shelf above the stack of gold. "What is that?" she asked while pointing.

"Well, let's see," Marsha said as she pulled out a stack of papers.

"Maps," said Segal, as she quickly looked at Cohen.

"Let's see. Four maps in total," Marsha replied as they were placed in a large plastic bag, marked, and placed in a cardboard box labeled the same way. "Looks like a journal or diary as well," Marsha added. She started pulling it off the top of the safe, but then put it back, asking one of her techs for another plastic bag.

22

CHAPTER

As THE SEARCH continued, Jeannie asked how Marsha was going to get the gold bars outside. "One brick at a time, I guess. Old Bob here has been working out, right, Bob? He should be able to handle it. We need to count all this currency, sign off on it, and seal it in a few boxes."

"I have a better idea. Let me contact Lomax and have him arrange for an armored car to transport the gold and currency to your office. Will your safe handle all of this?"

"If not, you can drop it off at my house," she said while laughing. "No, your idea works for me. In fact, I hope he can come up with a plan to transport the gold, currency, jewels, and paintings, so I only need to handle the maps, diary, and the rest of the smaller items."

Jeannie called Lomax and asked for suggestions about how to securely transport everything that had been found. He became just as excited about the find as Jeannie was. He told her he would get back to her.

"Alright, I guess we just wait until the calvary arrives," Marsha said to her techs. Their conversation, laughter, and banter concealed the sound of the approach from individuals who had crept in below. Jeannie could not remember how the gunfire started. The gunmen burst into the room where everyone was still gathered and looking at various items. They said nothing but just started firing.

Jeannie saw Ismail get hit several times, falling to the floor before he could pull out his weapon. Jeannie could not hear due to the deafening gunshots that filled the room. She pulled out her weapon but then felt a sharp pain in her left arm. A second round hit her on her forehead, knocking her unconscious. The gunmen grabbed the cardboard box labeled with maps and diary and quickly left the residence.

An hour and a half later, Jeannie woke in a hospital gown with her head bandaged. She had an IV in her right arm and felt a stinging sensation in her left. "Welcome back to the living," a male nurse said to Jeannie. At first, her vision was blurred, but she regained her focus and stared at the nurse. "Try not to move too much. As you can tell, you have an IV going, and you have been sedated. Let me go get the doctor."

"Wait. What about my partner and the other people in the room?" Jeannie asked, but the nurse either ignored her or did not hear her question. She tried to remember what had happened. It all happened so quickly. Everyone, including Marsha and her techs, was looking at all the valuables they had found in the room. She could not wait to get back to the office and review the maps and, especially, the diary. *How many gunmen were there? What did they look like? How did they know we were there? Think Jeannie, think.*

"How do you feel?" a female doctor asked when she entered the room. Jeannie saw her identification badge. Sharon Friedman, M.D.

"Fine, doctor. Can you tell me about my partner, Agent Flores, and the other people in the room?"

"Let's focus on you," she said.

"No, God damn it. I said I'm fine and I need to know how everyone else is. Now, either you tell me, or (she attempted to pull out her IV)…."

"Alright. Your supervisor is waiting to see you. He can answer your questions, but you need to leave the IV in place for now. You received a blow to your forehead from a bullet, but it only grazed you. To be on the safe side, I've ordered an MRI to make sure there is no internal damage. You will have a scar, but a plastic surgeon should easily clean it up. Your left arm got a through-and-though, but fortunately, it did not hit an artery or do any muscular damage. You were extremely lucky. Let me get your supervisor."

"How do you feel?" was the first thing Lomax asked as he entered the room.

"Like I told the doctor, I am fine. How is Ismail and everyone else that was in the room? Do we know who the suspects are?"

Lomax approached the bed but did not sit on it. "Ismail is in bad shape. He took one in the chest and one in his side, but the worst was a bullet that entered his skull. He has been in surgery since they brought everyone in. He has a 50/50 chance of making it."

Jeannie felt salty tears running down her cheeks. "Oh, my God. He has to make it. He has a family. I need to get out of here. They need my support."

Lomax grabbed her good hand as she was attempting to remove her IV again. "Jeannie, stop. Ismail's wife is receiving support from family members in the waiting room. You are not in any shape to do anything but care for yourself."

"What about Segal, Cohen, and Marsha and her techs?"

"Segal and Cohen are also in surgery, but their wounds are not life-threatening. Sadly, Marsha and her team did not make it." Jeannie continued to cry and did not try to hide her emotions. She could not envision working without Ismail by her side. She turned away from Lomax and let her pillow absorb the moisture from her tears. After a few moments of silence, she regained her composure and turned to Lomax.

"Who did this? I suppose they took all the gold and other valuables. It's my fault. I should have thought about the house being watched. I just assumed our

Mossad agents were the ones we had to watch. I mean, Ismail and I had concluded they were responsible for the attempted burglary. Because of my blindness, my friend is possibly dying." The tears returned in earnest.

Lomax held Jeannie's hand. "Look, it is easy for me to say don't beat yourself up, but this is not who you are. Ismail is a fighter. If anyone can overcome these types of injuries, it is him. Hell, he will come out of it and start bragging about his scars. You'll see." Jeannie found herself smiling after his comments.

"Neighbors who heard the shots say there were six gunmen. They saw them leaving the house carrying a cardboard box. An armored car had just driven up at the same time. Three guards got out of the back to get the gold. That is one more than they normally have, but due to the amount of property, the guard service ordered an extra man. The gunmen surprised them, killing not only them but the driver who got out to help."

"Jesus. It's that God damn Organization."

They appear to have only taken one box outside of the hidden room. No gold bars are missing. They left everything else behind. They were only interested in one box for some reason. Sid McDonald and his forensic team inventoried what was left behind, and the items are now in our large safe on the evidence floor."

Jeannie processed what Lomax had said. "They were after the maps and diary. They weren't interested in a few bars of gold. They want to know the location of the gold train. I remember Marsha labeling one of the cardboard boxes with maps and diary. That's what they wanted. I should have thought of that."

23

CHAPTER

THREE DAYS LATER, Jeannie was officially released from the hospital. She had been given instructions by the doctor to start her medication the second she got home or suffer the consequences of a splitting headache and throbbing arm. She was to return in one week to have the stitches removed from her wounds. Jeannie listened to her doctor's advice but could not wait to get to the waiting room and learn about Ismail.

His wife saw her when she entered the room. She embraced Jeannie, and they both began to cry. Lomax stood, giving up his seat so the two could sit down together. "I'm so sorry. How is he doing?" Jeannie asked.

"The doctor said the surgery went well, but they will not know for another 24 hours. They have him in an induced coma right now. Jeannie, what am I going to do if I lose him? He is the only man I ever loved. And, what about our children? They need their father."

Jeannie continued to stroke her hand and offered words of comfort, but she was overcome with guilt.

Why did I just focus on the two Mossad agents? Those bastards want the gold to further their plans for the Fourth Reich.

"You should be home in bed," she said to Jeannie.

"No, he needs me here. What did the doctor tell you?" Jeannie asked.

"One of the bullets somehow damaged his liver and caused a lung to collapse. The second bullet in his side did no damage, but one entered his skull. The surgeon confided in me that they were able to remove the bullets, but with this kind of injury, the force of the projectile makes the prognosis nothing more than a guess. Jeannie, they had to open him up twice due to swelling in his head." She started to cry again and was joined by Jeannie.

"Even if he makes it, they are not sure whether there will be any permanent damage. All we can do now is pray." She collapsed into Jeannie's arms. Family members rushed to help Jeannie, who told them she needed to go home and that she would be notified if there were any changes. The final comment Jeannie heard while they were leaving was a relative saying, "Oh my God. Is he going to make it?"

***

"What do you mean there are only maps? Where's the diary? The maps are useless unless we have his diary."

"Sir, we found a box that the FBI had labeled maps and diary, so we took it. How were we to know the diary was not inside?"

"You should all be shot for your incompetence." After his tirade against Rictner, Heiliger hung up his phone. "The fucking FBI has the diary. We should have made sure we killed all those assholes," Rictner said.

***

Agent Shawn Warner drove Jeannie home after she had been given strict orders from Lomax to take a few days off work. He would call her if there were any further updates on Ismail's condition.

Warner and Jeannie only engaged in small talk on the drive. Warner had only recently been assigned to the San Francisco office, and they had not spent any time with each other. Thank God, Jeannie thought to herself, at least she didn't ask me how I was feeling. Jeannie thanked her once they arrived at her home. She carried her small bag of medicine in and was in the process of opening her front door when she heard Delores and Walter approach.

"Oh my God, Jeannie, are you alright? We heard on the news about the big shootout in San Francisco. I called the FBI and told them who I was, but they would not give me any information. You could have been killed. Walter, go home and bring the soup and bread."

"I'm okay, Delores, really. You don't need to have Walter bring me soup. I think I will just lie down and get some sleep. The meds (holding up the bag) make me really sleepy."

"Nonsense. I will not take no for an answer, young lady. As soon as I heard you had been shot but was okay, I made you some soup and fresh sourdough. I kept them in the refrigerator, but after you pop them in the microwave, they will be great. You need to build up your strength. Do you know who the assholes are that did this to you?"

Jeannie knew she couldn't win a debate with Delores, and she started to feel a headache coming on. She opened her front door, and she and Delores entered. As Jeannie was about to shut the door, Walter came walking up with a large pot of soup and a large loaf of sourdough bread. Delores took the bread from him and told him to put the pot on the stove.

"Now, why don't you lay down on your sofa and get some sleep? When you wake up, you will have a nice bowl of soup and bread waiting. If you have any problems, just call us. Remember, we both have concealed weapon permits and are not afraid to protect you. We are not going anywhere, are we, Walter?" *Don't know if that makes me feel safe or if I will have a nightmare thinking about that.*

Jeannie thanked them both and did as Delores suggested. She took her pills and then curled up on her couch, covering herself with a blanket. She tried to remember everything about the shooting, but the medication kicked in, and it did not take long for her to fall into a deep sleep.

When she woke up, she saw that she had slept for almost four hours. It was near 5 p.m. She checked her cell phone and found no messages. Remembering the soup and sourdough that Delores and Walter had brought, she poured herself a bowl of soup and cut two slices of bread. She set the microwave for two-and-a-half minutes on high and waited. She looked at the bottles of medication to see how often she was supposed to take them. The soup and sourdough really hit the spot.

Finishing her meal, she fed her fish and told them what she could remember about the shootout. They did not seem impressed at all. *See if I share anything in the future with you guys.* She walked upstairs, noticing that each step seemed to cause a reaction in her forehead.

Easy does it, girl. She tried to maneuver the bandages on her forehead to see how bad it looked, but it was put on too securely, and her head already hurt from climbing the stairs. She heard her phone ring and realized it was downstairs. Not thinking, she quickly started back down the stairs when a light bolt flashed in her eyes, and her forehead began to throb. *Slow down, damn it.*

When she reached the phone, she saw that it was a scam call. She put it in her pocket. She did some channel surfing but found nothing that interested her, so back upstairs and into bed she went. *Maybe tomorrow will bring a better outlook on the events of the past week.*

A little after 8 a.m., her phone rang again. *Better not be scam.* Checking the phone ID, it was Lomax. "How is he?" she immediately asked.

"No change, but that might be a good sign. Cohen and Segal have been released. I met some other individuals who are going to care for them. They identified themselves as coming from the Israel embassy, but I smell more Mossad. Cohen took one in the leg and one in the shoulder. The leg was the worst. He will be on crutches for a little while.

Segal got hit in the neck, just missing her carotid. Another round caught her in the right arm. She will also be out of action for a few weeks at least. Forensics pretty much destroyed the inside of the house, searching for any more secret rooms, but nothing else was found. How are you healing?"

"Had a bad night with a massive headache even with the meds, but I feel pretty good this morning except for my arm itching already. Do you think maybe someone can come and pick me up and take me to the office since my car is still there and I am without wheels?"

"Absolutely not," he replied, stretching out the a-b-s-o-l-u-t-e-l-y and making her think he was going to agree. "If I remember correctly, your doctor said you are not to drive for a few days."

"The doctor feels you need two weeks off. We can handle things here until your return. Contrary to some people's beliefs, I think I am still young enough to multitask. Besides, what can you do here? The trail is cold. We have all the property secured here in our building. Those guys would be fools to try a stunt here like they did at the house."

"How about this? Would it be possible for someone to email me a list of the property indexed by McDonald's forensic team? I want to see everything they left behind."

"I guess we can do that, but not until tomorrow. You still need rest. Let me see if either McDonald or even Burk or Darcy are free to send it to you. Give me a few." With that, he hung up.

24

CHAPTER

JEANNIE NAPPED OFF and on. She had a hard time going back to sleep the previous evening, probably due to all her cat naps. She got up at 5:30 in the evening and looked at what was still displayed on her upstairs bedroom wall. *Need to update this with what has transpired.* Her thoughts were interrupted by a knock on her front door. *Has to be Delores.*

Sure enough, there stood Delores in a flower-patterned bathrobe with her hair in curlers, carrying a plastic quart-size container with food items. "Oh, hi, Jeannie. I wanted to check to see how you were feeling. Did you like the soup?

"The soup was amazing, and the bread, wow. Did you make it yourself?"

"No, Walter made the bread. I made the soup. He took a class at Chabot College on bread making. He's pretty good at it. Any information about who shot you? How are the other agents who were shot?"

Good old Delores, the woman of rapid questions. "Sadly, my partner is not out of danger."

"Oh, my God, I hope he makes it."

"As do we all. I'm sure you heard it on the news, but three of my colleagues were killed. They were not agents but forensics technicians gathering evidence when they were shot. Four security guards were also killed. Besides my partner, two people from Israel were injured, but they will recover."

"Israel? That must have been some investigation." *Delores is fishing. I love it, but I will not bite.*

"What do you have here?" Jeannie asked, looking at the plastic container Delores was holding.

"Oh, I almost forgot. I made Walter some French toast and bacon for breakfast, and I made some for you. You need to nourish your body to get healthy. There are also two turkey sandwiches in there for lunch, so you don't have to go out." She handed the box to Jeannie. "Do you need me to come in and feed your fish?"

"Gee, Delores, this is so nice of you. You and Walter are the best neighbors a single gal could ask for. Thanks for the offer, but the doctor told me to walk around so I can feed the koi myself, but again, thanks." Just then, her phone went off in her pocket. She looked at the ID. "I'm so sorry, Delores. I really need to take this call. It might be about my partner." Delores had hoped to just stand there and hear parts of the conversation, but Jeannie shut the front door, feeling bad in the process.

"Jeannie. He's going to make it," Lomax said. The doctor just told me that his vitals are back to normal. They will still keep him in a coma and monitor any swelling in his brain, but it looks like he will pull through."

"Thank God!" She started to cry. "How is his wife holding up?"

"The doctor told her the same good news, and she has finally given in to his request to return home and get more sleep. There is nothing she can do for Ismail at the hospital. Darcy said she sent the email to you. Did you receive it?"

"Damn, I forgot all about it. I'm sure I got it. I'll check now. Thank you for calling me, and say hi to everyone. Oh, and please thank them for the lovely bouquet of flowers and candy that were delivered." She checked her computer upstairs and found the email from Darcy. "Everyone hopes you will get well soon. The attachment contains all the evidence inventoried by forensics."

Before bringing up the attachment, Jeannie decided to take a long hot bath. She'd been told to avoid getting her head and arm wet, so a bath seemed to be the way to go. Her hair would be in a mess in a few days, but a female nurse at the hospital had told her about a product that didn't need water. It was a non-rinse shampoo and conditioner. *I must pick some up if I ever get my car back.*

Feeling much better after the bath, clothed in her sweats and bathrobe, and with a cup of coffee in hand, she opened the file. *Huh. Those assholes left all the gold bars and paintings, even the Picasso and Rembrandt. They wanted the maps and diary.* Jeannie's heart jumped. There, on the final page of the attachment, was item 81: an apparent diary. Jeannie remembered that Marsha was going to remove it from the top of the safe but needed a plastic bag from her crew. *Thank you, Marsha.*

Jeannie quickly got dressed and called a car rental agency that, for an additional fee, would deliver your rental car to your home. Less than an hour later, a college-aged Black male arrived at her door to deliver a blue Volkswagen Jetta. After the t's were crossed and i's dotted, Jeannie was on her way to the office. She thought of letting Delores and Walter know, but that would waste time. The Jetta did not perform like her Corvette, but it provided a comfortable ride into the city.

As soon as she got off the elevator, she was greeted by applause or "welcome back" from everyone she ran into until Lomax came around the corner to see what all the racket was about. "What are you doing here?" he asked, but before she explained, he pointed to his office. *Uh oh. Ass chewing time.*

"Did I or didn't I give you a direct order to take two weeks off as prescribed by your doctor?"

"Yes, you did, but technically, if I am given credit for time served in the hospital, there is only about one week left regarding my rehab. I could not stay at home knowing that we are sitting on a vital document that could break the case wide open." She could tell that Lomax was still not a happy camper.

"This better be good," he said.

Jeannie opened her purse and pulled out printed copies of the inventory sent to her by Darcy. She handed it to Lomax. "Look at item recorded as number 81."

He stared hard at Jeannie while putting on his reading glasses and then turned his attention to the paper. "I'll be damned. The son-of-a-bitch did keep a diary."

"Yes. I now remember Marsha finding it at the top of that massive safe. She was going to put it in the same cardboard box as the maps but then asked one of her techs for a plastic evidence bag, and then the shooting started."

25

CHAPTER

JEANNIE SIGNED THE diary out from the evidence locker and promised Lomax that she would drive right home and start her rehab while examining it. On the ride back, she kept glancing at the large black book, wondering what secrets it contained.

"CAN I HELP you?" called Delores before she recognized that it was Jeannie getting out of the Jetta. "Oh, hi, Jeannie. I didn't recognize the car, and I didn't want you to be disturbed. Should you be driving in your condition?" Jeannie noticed a bulge on Delores' hip that was covered by her sweater. *Old girl must be packing heat.*

Jeannie was civil and friendly and, after a short time, managed to escape her "interrogator" and got into her house. She went upstairs and changed back into her sweats and t-shirt. Back downstairs, she grabbed one of the remaining turkey sandwiches that Delores had brought over and a diet Dr. Pepper. She put on a pair of plastic gloves and positioned the diary on a table away from her tray with her food and drink. Sitting cross-legged, she pulled the diary from the plastic evidence bag and opened it on page one. It had been a long time since she had taken German in high school and college, but Detwrick's writing was very legible and easy to read.

Dacha, Germany
April 3, 1941

Today is my first day here at the Dacha camp. I am about 12 km from Munich. This camp serves as a prototype and model for the other concentration camps and SS officers are sent here for our initial training. The prisoner's portion of the camp covers five hectares. The prisoner enclosure at the camp is heavily guarded to ensure that no prisoners escape. There is a much larger area for our SS training school and our barracks plus factories and other facilities that expand the camp to around twenty hectares.

It is here in our school that I will be taught to adapt as an officer of the Waffen SS and become capable of performing any task given to me when assigned to a concentration camp. My training could take as long as nineteen months. I will be taught map reading, tactics, military maneuvers, political education, weapons training, physical education, combat engineering and even automobile mechanics. I know it will be a challenge, but that is why I chose to join the SS.

Dacha, Germany
April 17, 1941

Today marks two weeks of my studies. I am both proud and sad at my number two ranking in my class standings. Soon, I will be number one. I have no doubt what-so-ever. Cocky bastard, Jeannie thought. *Today, we were shown how the gassing of prisoners is to be done. I did not realize how much preparation is necessary to kill the Jews. It was stressed that when transport trains arrive at the various extermination camps, all efforts to trick the Jews must be incorporated.*

One such technique that has proven helpful is the playing of music upon their arrival. Then we have specially selected Jews who operate like porters, helping the Jews out of the cars and hanling them tickets, telling them not to lose them so they can be reunited with their belongings after their shower. Of course, they will never see their luggage again. This applies to all their valuables. Some think they are being clever and hide their valuables in their mouths or their underwear or even up their asses. These vermin have stolen from and lived off Germans for far too long.

In some camps, they are given postcards so they can write to loved ones about their safe arrival. Once they write on the cards, they are collected and mailed for them. We believe that this news will spread through the Jewish communities, thus continuing to hide what we have planned for them.

Also today, I killed my first Jew. I was walking with Sergeant Wagner when a female Jew started walking past us. He ordered her to stop and looked at me. Have you killed a Jew yet? He asked. I told him no. He ordered me to shoot her. I looked at her, but she looked down at the ground. I pulled out my sidearm and armed it at her head. My sergeant told me to shoot her between her eyes so she would die instantly. I told her to look at me and when she did, I pulled the trigger. She fell to the ground, and we walked on.

Jeannie closed the diary. With misty eyes, she began walking towards her kitchen, lost in thought. She remembered watching a lot of History Channel presentations with her dad about the atrocities the Nazis committed in the death camps, but to read it from a person who was being trained in the butchery of human beings was just plain horrific. Visions of the movie *Schindler's List* came to mind, and she thought of all the innocent children, including babies, that were sent to their deaths. She poured a cup of coffee, and after doctoring it up with Cremora and Truvia, she returned to the couch. She reopened the diary and found where she had left off.

When the Jews arrive, it is best to separate women and children of a certain age from the males. We call it separating the herd. The infirm are initially put beside the women and later loaded onto wagons or other means of transportation and taken to the changing room. It is recommended to march the males off first, and then the females and children, followed by the weak.

Once they enter the changing room, they are told to hang up their clothes and remember the number displayed above its hook. They are told to tie their shoes together, so they do not get lost. It is all a lie, but they don't realize it. They are too ignorant. If you are dealing with males, from here they are led to the gas chamber or, as we tell them, the showers.

Women are treated a little differently before entering the gas chamber. They have their hair cut off after being told that typhus and lice needed to be controlled. Next, off they go to the shower room where, thirty or so minutes later, they have been gassed. This time varies depending on whether Zyklon-B gas or diesel exhaust is used.

I found the lectures today quite stimulating. I was told by my superior that in three-weeks, my training will focus on my duties and responsibilities when assigned to my first concentration camp.

Jeannie stopped reading. *A fucking sociopath.* She finished her sandwich, soda, and coffee and returned to the diary. She thumbed through more of his earlier writings which continued with his ramblings about training and his SS indoctrination.

May 2, 1941
Auschwitz

I am honored to have been assigned here to Auschwitz – Birkenau, the largest of the extermination centers in the Reich. It is two camps plus forty sub camps. The older portion, Auschwitz I, was initially meant to serve as a detention center for political prisoners. Later, it became overcrowded when Jews began being transported here, so Auschwitz II, or Birkenau, was built.

My commandant is Rudolf Höss, who had previously helped run the Sachsenhausen concentration camp in Oranienburg, Germany. He was dispatched to evaluate the feasibility of establishing a concentration camp here in western Poland. It was his favorable report that led to the creation of Auschwitz, and his appointment as its commandant.

I think he is about 5'8"and of average weight. His wife's name is Hedwig, and they have five children.

I am fortunate to be here at this camp since it is gearing up to process the death of more Jews than any of the other camps. In fact, the majority now being transported here are Jews. When they arrive here, the detainees are examined by Nazi doctors. One of our doctors, Josef Mengele, is conducting research on twins so those are generally the first selected. He is doing great work in the medical field using Jews as subjects of his experiments.

For example, to study eye color, he injects colored dye into the eyeballs of twins to see if it transfers over to their identical match. He also injects chloroform into the hearts of twins to determine if both siblings die at the same time and in the same manner. I find this quite fascinating.

During what we call the selection process, those Jews considered unfit for work, including young children, the elderly, pregnant women, and the infirm, are immediately ordered to the showers. However, the bathhouses to which they are marched are disguised gas chambers.

Once inside, the prisoners are exposed to Zyklon-B poison gas which we use here instead of diesel exhaust gas. Once they are sealed inside the gas chamber, an SS soldier wearing a gas mask opens a vent on the roof and pours the Zyklon-B pellets onto the floor where, when exposed to oxygen, they turn into a deadly gas. We found this is a very effective way to kill rats. Individuals marked as unfit for work are never officially registered as Auschwitz inmates. They go directly to the gas chamber.

I was told that, before I was stationed here, we only transported a relatively small number of Jews who were sent here along with non-Jewish prisoners, mostly Poles, who accounted for most the camp's population until mid-1942. Now, it seems, we have trains coming several times each day so we must be efficient. Jeannie shook her head in disbelief.

May 4, 1941
Auschwitz

Today, I ordered the replacement of Sonderkommandos 5. The new group will need time to pick up speed in their duties. Something unusual happened in gas chamber 3. When the Sonderkommandos went in after gassing to pull the bodies apart and check for gold and silver fillings, they found a young girl still alive. From what Karl told me, the eleven-year-old ended up at the bottom of a pile of bodies and her head was partially in a pool of water, or urine, I can't remember. Anyway, this prevented her full inhalation of gas and she survived. Well, she survived the gassing, but Karl shot her after walking her to the crematorium.

Jeannie flipped through more of the diary and ended up on the entry for January 2, 1942.

Treblinka
January 2, 1942

I have been ordered by Reichsführer Himmler to inspect the railroad lines leading to this camp. It is in a forest north-east of Warsaw, about 4 km south of the village of Treblinka. It has only been operational for one month. There are two camps here. Treblinka 1 is a forced-labor camp where the prisoners work in the gravel pit or irrigation area, and in the forest where they cut wood to fuel the cremation pits.

Treblinka is one of our most productive camps. 700,000 and 900,000 Jews have been murdered in our gas chambers, along with 2,000 Romanians. In fact, more Jews have been murdered here than at any other Nazi extermination camp, apart from Auschwitz-Birkenau. That is very impressive.

Jeannie got up and walked to her fish tank. "Very impressive. Very impressive!" she yelled. "What a sick fuck you were, Detwrick. I hope you are rotting in hell." Her fish apparently agreed, she thought, since they rose to the top of their home waiting for some extra food pellets, which they received. After venting, she returned to the diary.

The second camp, Treblinka II, is the extermination camp. The way this camp was originally laid out, with there being two camps, makes modifications to the railroad line very challenging.

Sobibor
April 7, 1942

Today, I was chosen by the commandant to supervise laying a new railroad line towards the entrance to Sobibor camp. We had a near riot a week ago when a group of Jews attempted to flee after getting out of the cattle cars. We dispatched them easily, but the commandant said it must never happen again. Before that, we also caught several Jews trying to hide in the piles of clothing that were being shipped back to Germany. These Jews are very sneaky.

I walked around the front entrance of the camp a few weeks ago, and concluded that if the railroad track made a turn into the camp and then a gate was closed before the Jews were taken off the train, their escape route would be removed. My extension of the railroad track would allow for the entire train, including the engine, to enter the camp and then, with the gate closed and guards in place, the Jews would be allowed to exit the cars. After they were escorted out of the immediate area, the gate could then be opened and the train could exit. I drew up my plans for the track extension and showed them to the commandant who signed off on the idea, but I have heard nothing more about my plan.

Jeannie closed the diary, wondering how many citizens not only in the United States, but the world, knew of the mechanism of death employed by the Nazis. She knew there were idiots among us that denied the entire Holocaust event, but with history not being taught in our schools and universities, and with students more interested in social media and the latest video games, she doubted many had any idea of the mass murders.

26

CHAPTER

NIGHTMARES AFFECTED JEANNIE'S sleep to the point when she got up at 1 a.m., poured herself a strong cup of coffee, and returned to the diary.

Sobibor
December 30, 1942

It has been a while since I made an entry, but so much has happened lately I have not had time to write. The war on the eastern front is not going well. The weather has taken a turn for the worse and our troops are freezing and starving to death near Stalingrad. I am afraid the war will now come to us.

Two days ago, a group of Jews assigned to hard labor tried to escape. They first knocked out a Ukrainian guard at a stream where two Jews had gone to get water. When they did not return, a second guard went to check, discovering the escape. No doubt inspired by this, the remaining eleven Jews took off in different directions. It did not matter. They were all captured, including the first two who made it to a farm. The farmer turned them in for a reward.

All thirteen were returned to the camp. I thought the commandant would just execute them, but he ordered something different. He assembled all the Jews in the center of the compound, even those Jews who were working in the kitchen preparing the day's next meal. The thirteen stood before the group. Instead of just machine gunning them down as a message, he forced them to go out among the assembled crowd and select a person to die with them that day. At first, they refused, but then he gave them an alternative. If they did not go and select a partner in death, then he would select 50. He pointed out the mathematics involved. Either 26 would die, or 50. The choice was up to them. Twenty-six died. A very impressive message, I felt.

Jeannie stopped reading, feeling nauseous. *God, how could you allow something like this to happen?*

Sobibor
February 1, 1943

While on patrol this afternoon, I visited the kitchen area to check on the Jews preparing dinner. This was not the normal time for my inspection. When I walked in, I found one of the Jews eating, and he quickly shoved something into his pocket.

"What are you doing, you filthy Jew? I asked. He said nothing, like they mostly do. I asked him to empty his

pocket where I saw him put something. Sheepishly, he did, showing me a slice of bread. I ordered him to lay down on the floor and pulled out my pistol. I placed the barrel on the back of his head and pulled the trigger, but it mis fired. I looked at my weapon and saw that it had stove-piped. I cleared the bad round, rechambered a new round, and then shot him. I wonder what was going through his mind while I fixed my gun?

Sobibor
February 2, 1943

I was ordered to the commandant's office early this morning. My plans for the extension of the railroad line for Sobibor were accepted by Himmler himself. He even sent a note of congratulations! In more good news, Himmler showed my plans to Reichmarschall Goering who was also very impressed. He attached a note to Himmler's congratulations stating that he planned to visit me and see my work in the near future.

Tomorrow, we will start laying the track. I hope to have it completed by next week at the latest.

Sobibor
April 4, 1943

Reichmarschall Goering, after congratulating me in person and presenting me with a medal, had me walk with him outside away from others while acting as if he was looking at the recently laid rails. He told me in strict confidence that I would soon be transferred to a post in Austria. The exact location would be revealed later. This caught Jeannie's attention.

He told me what I had already surmised. The war was going badly in Russia, and it appeared the tide was changing. He had been instructed by our Führer to start the immediate transportation and relocation of the goods seized from the Jews to be used in the future if the Third Reich was not successful in winning the war. If that were to happen, Hitler wanted to ensure the new Fourth Reich would arise.

Of course, I knew of the collection of valuables we seized when the Jews arrived here. They try to hide their valuables, but we always find them. Sometimes, we find them in their shit and have to get another Jew to wash off their filth before we can collect them. I have collected quite a bit for myself for after the war along with my colleagues. We know that if we are caught it would mean the Russian front, or worse, our execution, but since everyone is doing it, the changes of being turned in make it worthwhile. I don't know how much treasure I have, but soon, I will need a new hiding place.

My orders were to be kept confidential from other SS personnel, including the commandant. I will be supervising the construction of a secret tunnel and railroad line leading to it, and the arrival and seclusion of our Führer's gold train. What an honor.

First, he will arrange for my transfer to Ravensbruck concentration camp for a short time so my co-workers will not link me to my top-secret assignment. Later, he will arrange for another transfer, but this will be false since I am to remain in Austria with the train assignment.

Jeannie closed the diary. There it was. The motive behind the Organization and the attack on Detwrick's home. Somehow, like Mossad, they had learned of Detwrick possessing either maps and/or this diary. They are willing to kill anyone who gets in their way of securing the location of the gold train and its contents. She picked up the phone and called Lomax.

***

"Sir, we have gone over and over these maps, and without Detwrick's diary, we only know that the train is located somewhere in Austria; at least, all the maps are of that country," Rictner told Heiliger on the phone.

"He did not circle the area where the train is concealed? Then what the hell good are the maps?"

"I can only guess that he used the maps to study the location of the railroad lines in the immediate area and the best route to come off them leading to the tunnel, but he never wrote specific directions on the maps." No one spoke for several seconds. "Are you still there, sir?"

"Yes, I am still here. Where the fuck do you think I would be? I am thinking… Alright, I think it is safe to assume the train is somewhere in Austria. You three fly there and wait for instructions. The Organization will continue to monitor the FBI's movements. If they arrive anywhere in Austria, we will mobilize our forces and intercept them once they lead us to the train."

27

CHAPTER

"Agent Lomax, my name is Samuel Goldman." Goldman offered his hand to Lomax after being escorted to the SAC's office. I wanted to personally thank you for looking out for the immediate medical care of Ariel Segal and Levi Cohen. I realize that your organization lost three outstanding individuals. May I ask how your agents Loomis and Flores are doing?"

Lomax studied Goldman. He felt he was near his age, but in much better shape. Maybe 6'2" and 175 pounds, broad-shouldered with a thick head of brown hair speckled with gray. Dressed in a three-piece suit, Lomax knew he, too, was a Mossad agent.

He also knew that Mossad would be sending replacements. With the information sent to Israel about what was found in Detwrick's residence and the existence of maps and a diary, they needed to stay in the game.

"Agent Flores is out of intensive care but will need a lot of physical therapy. I heard however, that he is driving the nurses crazy. Agent Loomis is on the mend."

Goldman smiled. After a moment of silence, he smoothed his pants leg and revealed why he was there. As Lomax had anticipated, he was asking if two replacements for Segal and Cohen could be allowed to continue with the FBI's investigation.

"I assume they have been cleared by Washington?"

"They have, but I am sure you will check. Their names are Eleazar Lieberman and Joseph Alderman. Both are very capable agents and have been appraised regarding the status of the investigation. I was also wondering if you have any information to share since the tragic shooting?"

"And you, Mr. Goldman, have you been cleared by Washington? No offense."

"None taken. Please, if you do not have the number Cohen and Segal gave you, here is the number again. He handed the card to Lomax, who just put it in his shirt pocket.

"Last I checked Israel and the US are allies, therefore we should continue to share what we know. We are still allies, aren't we?" Lomax asked with a smile on his face.

"Agent Lomax, sometimes my nation watches the news from your country, and when we see and hear people like those in a group called the 'Squad,' we wonder not only how these individuals got elected but also how many in the United States share their values and ideology?"

"Believe me, Mr. Goldman, their constituents are very small in number, and they do not represent anything close to the sentiment of most US citizens. I agree with you, and often wonder how they ever got elected, but it seems recently that their time in the spotlight is about over. I failed to ask how your two agents are doing?"

"Both of them have flown home to Tel Aviv. Cohen will be in a leg cast for about three weeks but is healing well. Segal is ahead of Cohen regarding complete recovery. Thank you for asking. I will pass on your concerns to them both."

"Please do. Now, as we say here in the States, let's address the elephant in the room. You want to know about Detwrick's diary. First, the items found in the room after our agents were attacked are stored here in our vault. I can share the list with you." He picked up the phone and asked Darcy to bring down a copy of the evidence log from the Grant Street house. He turned and faced Goldman. "Now, the diary is in the possession of Agent Loomis."

"Yes, of course, Agent Loomis. My agents were very impressed with her leadership and the respect she receives from her subordinates."

"Yes. Jeannie, I mean Agent Loomis, is an outstanding agent. God willing, she will take over my position here in the future. She called me last night.

She is only part way through Detwrick's writings. Let's get a coffee and I will fill you in on what she has read so far. I also want to ask you some questions about the Organization."

Jeannie stopped at an In-and-Out Burger and bought a double-double, fries, and a chocolate shake for take-out. She was still driving her rental and needed to figure out how to get rid of it and get her car from the bureau. Arriving at the hospital, the smell from the burger joint had filled the rental car making her hungry. *Should have bought one for yourself, dummy.*

"Some guys get all the breaks, don't they?" Jeannie asked Ismail's wife as she entered his room. She gave Jeannie a long, loving hug. "How's the pain-in-the-ass doing?"

"Once again, I am in the room. Hey, boss, what's in the bag? Could that be something for me?"

"Yeah, it's for you, but if the nurses catch you with it, I will take the fifth."

"Give me, give me, give me," Ismail said with both of his arms outstretched.

"Here, mi amor. Let me get your tray so you don't spill anything on yourself."

"That's okay. The night shift nurse is going to give me a sponge bath tonight and she is hot." His wife looked at Jeannie and shook her head.

"You were right. We should have arranged for a shrink to come in and examine him."

Jeannie talked with Ismail's wife as he inhaled the burger and fries. Jeannie could not blame him. The food she ate when she was here was bland to say the least. She asked about the kids, their schooling, and again asked how she was doing with the pain-in-the-ass?

"Again, I am here. You know, I almost got my ass shot off by a bunch of Nazis, and do I get any sympathy from my boss? No, only a lousy, stinking hamburger. All those years covering for her in the field and look what I get." He picked up his chocolate milk shake.

"Well, if you feel that way, I can finish your shake," Jeannie said, advancing towards his bed."

"No, No. I need it to get my strength back. I got some Nazis that need to be put down. Speaking of which, what's going on with the case?" His wife excused herself to use the restroom, and after she left, Jeannie closed the door.

"First, Lomax told me that both Segal and Cohen will be fine. They are both back in Israel recovering. Lomax went to Marsha's funeral and conveyed our sincere sympathy to the family. I had Darcy and Burk go to her techs' funerals, and the bureau did a great job at all their ceremonies. I'm not sure if the bureau sent anyone to armored car guards' funerals. I don't know how much you remember, Ace. I still have parts that are missing in my memory."

"Man, I have been racking my brain, but I can't remember shit. The doctor said it is short term amnesia brought on by the bullet entering a certain part of my brain. By the way, how do you like my new look? The head bandage makes me look like a Taliban terrorist, huh? That's me, Achmed the Terrorist." He laughed. "Anyway. he said that it should come back over time."

Jeannie brought Ismail up to speed. He was fascinated about the possibility of there actually being a gold train hidden in some tunnel somewhere. "I told the doctor I needed to get out of here as soon as possible since you need my expert investigation skills."

"You're not going anywhere," Jeannie said. "You almost got killed." She started to cry.

"Hey, don't go all Hallmark on me now," he said as his wife knocked and re-entered the room.

"Okay, mi amor, what did you do now?" she asked on seeing Jeannie crying.

28

CHAPTER

"WOULD YOU LIKE your coffee black or with cream and sugar?" Lomax asked Goldman once they reached the breakroom.

"Black would be fine. May I ask what the FBI knows about the Nazis?" *That's the oldest trick in the book, Lomax thought. If he revealed what they knew, Goldman would only fill in with bits and pieces.* Not playing the game, Lomax responded, "Let's approach it from the standpoint that we do not know anything about the Organization." Goldman, smiled.

"Of course. And when I am through, you will tell me what your Agent Loomis has read so far?"

"Agreed."

Goldman took a deep breath, unbuttoned the top button of his collar and pulled the tie away from his neck. "Much better. The Organization does not really have a start date. Plans had already been put in place by Hitler when he realized the war was lost. Of course, many Nazis came to that conclusion years before Hitler admitted it and were making plans to jump ship, maybe sailing to South America where many of them landed."

"Who started the Organization is also pure speculation. Some suggest it was Hermann Goering and it started after Hitler placed him in charge of supervising the safe storage of property taken from the victims of the Holocaust. Others think it was Martin Bormann. We may never know."

"When the war was nearly over, Hitler ordered his scorched earth policy, but Goering, along with Albert Speer, refused to carry it out. Of course, fanatical members of the SS continued with Hitler's plan."

"You see, Goering's standing with Hitler and the German public declined after the Luftwaffe proved incapable of preventing the Allied bombing of German cities and resupplying of the surrounded Axis forces in Stalingrad. Around that time, Goering increasingly withdrew from military and political affairs to devote his attention to collecting property and artwork, much of which was stolen from Jews."

"Informed on April 22, 1945 that Hitler intended to commit suicide, Goering sent a telegram to Hitler requesting his permission to assume leadership of the Reich. Considering his request an act of treason, Hitler removed Goering from all his positions, expelled him from the party, and ordered his arrest."

"Now, Bormann is a different story. He wasn't as flamboyant and boisterous as Goering but he held immense power by using his position as Hitler's private secretary to control the flow of information and access to Hitler. He created an extensive bureaucracy and involved himself as much as possible in decision-making. He was part of Hitler's inner circle and accompanied him everywhere, providing briefings and summaries of events and requests."

"He had final approval over civil service appointments and reviewed and approved legislation and by 1943, he had *de facto* control over all domestic matters. Because of his high position in the party and with Hitler, he was in a similar position to Goering to oversee the future development of the Fourth Reich. Of course, we will never know."

"Yes, I know that Bormann returned with Hitler to the Führerbunker in Berlin on January 16, 1945, as the Red Army was closing its grip on Berlin. After Hitler committed suicide, Bormann and others attempted to flee Berlin to avoid capture by the Soviets. Most now agree that Bormann probably committed suicide on a bridge near Lehrter Station. His body was buried nearby on May 8, 1945 but was not found and confirmed as Bormann until 1973. The identification was reaffirmed in 1998 with DNA tests," Lomax said.

"Your history of World War II is very impressive," Goldman said.

"Yes, I have always been fascinated by that period of history. I majored in World History while in college but I still, to this day, cannot believe that the Nazis, especially Hitler, were capable of coming to power. But, then again, look at recent events like Iraq, a near duplicate of the Nazi government dictated over by Saddam Hussain." They both paused and played with their coffee cups.

"Regarding the structure of the Organization, they continue along the same lines as Himmler originally set up the SS. At formal gatherings, they all dress up in their SS uniforms that look identical to those worn during the war."

"The current head of the Organization is one Otto Heiliger. He is fifty-two years old. His father was German while his mother was Austrian. Both parents are dead. He has no brothers or sisters. He comes from a "proud" lineage of SS officers."

"His great-grandfather was stationed in Berlin and was highly trusted by Himmler. Later, he was assigned to SS General Reinhard Heydrick to assist in the formation of the death camps in Poland. He died in the bombings of Germany."

"Our agency does not know how many members are in the Organization. Since World War II, they have infiltrated almost all walks of life. Business, politics, you name it. They are international, with their primary goal being to create Hitler's dream of a Fourth Reich. I will arrange to have a list of known associates and their business or government positions sent to you.

The list is highly confidential. The Organization can never learn that we know where they are hidden, so to speak."

"Does Heiliger have a permanent location?"

"He moves around between five different countries and is heavily guarded. To our knowledge, he has not set up a location here in the United States."

"If you know where he is, I assume you have tried to eliminate him and his top staff?"

Goldman took a sip of his coffee, giving him time to formulate a response. "We have attempted, unsuccessfully, to eliminate him and the rest of the vipers, but their reach is far and wide, and he is always tipped off before we can act. Recently, he held a large gathering in Berlin to celebrate Hitler's birthday."

"April 20," Lomax said.

"That is correct. With all the top ghouls in one location, we felt one large explosion would chop off the head of the snake. The explosives were discovered, and the event was moved elsewhere. Agent Lomax, we are constantly monitoring our staff to make sure the Organization has not infiltrated our agency. That is how well organized it is."

***

After her visit with Ismail, Jeannie arranged with the rental car agency to pick up their car in San Francisco. After that was done, she called an Uber and was driven to the bureau to pick up her car without bumping into Lomax.

She stopped at the grocery store and picked up some items. Next, she hit a Subway store, and returned home. It was turning out to be a lucky day. She had avoided Lomax, and now she was safely in her home without Delores catching her. With her footlong sandwich, chips, and drink in hand, she began reading the diary where she had left off.

August 9, 1943
Mauthausen, Austria

When I first arrived at the camp, I was confused. Unlike Belzec, Sobibor, and Treblinka, this is one of the older extermination camps and its layout does not allow for expeditious railroad transports. This will take a lot of work.

I remember from my training in Dachau that in August 1938, the SS transferred the first prisoners from the Dachau concentration camp to here. During this phase, the prisoners, who were all male Germans and Austrians, had to build their own camp and set up operations in the quarry. Their daily lives were shaped by hunger, arbitrary treatment, and violence – nothing less than they deserved.

In December 1939, Himmler ordered the construction of a second concentration camp just a few kilometers from Mauthausen. This is where I am now stationed. It was in 1941 that the SS started to construct a gas chamber and other installations at Mauthausen for the systematic murder of large groups of Jews.

Later, several subcamps were created. Newly arriving prisoners were transferred to these camps from the main camp. More and more, Mauthausen itself became a camp where the sick and weak were sent to die.

I just received notification that puts my worries to rest. After I met with the Reichmarschall, I understood that my orders had nothing to do with Mauthausen. Instead, I have been given a top-secret assignment. Our Führer has given the Reichmarschall orders to start hiding valuables in the event of the Allied Forces advancing on the Third Reich. Our intelligence network has intercepted information of a possible Allied invasion. The valuables must not fall into the hands of our enemies.

September 12, 1943
Linz, Austria

The Reichmarschall returned to Berlin today after giving me a high-priority assignment. We had driven together from the Mauthausen camp to the base of the Salzkammergut Mountains, approximately 112 km from Linz. The highest peak, Mt. Gamsfeft, has an elevation of 2,027 meters and is near Gschütt Pass in the south. I am to construct an extension of the existing railroad system into a tunnel that I am also to build. I will have an unlimited supply of labor and funds to complete my task. Heil, Hitler!

Son-of-a bitch. Detwrick constructed a railroad line from Linz, Austria to a tunnel in the mountains. She searched for her phone and called Lomax. The call went to his voice mail. "Sir, call me ASAP. I know the general area where the train is located."

29

CHAPTER

JEANNIE FINISHED RE-READING the diary having made notes about the relevant points she would share with her team. She ran into a problem towards the back of the book that she needed to explain to Lomax. She received a return call from her doctor who gave her an early clearance to return to work, although it would be limited duty, whatever the hell that meant. She did have to check in with him for a final check and have her stitches removed. She called Lomax again.

"I was just going to call you," he said. "So, you think you know where the phantom gold train is located?"

"Not its exact location, but the general area, providing the information Detwrick wrote in his diary is not a bunch of bullshit. The problem is, when I thought he would start revealing specifics, Detwrick started using a code the closer he got to describing the mountain range, the location of the tunnel, and the train's exact location. His words make no sense. How do I explain this?"

"Let's say I start reciting a poem. 'Jack be nimble, Jack be quick,' and then I start saying, 'Isn't the weather great today?' It's like he placed random sentences and thoughts that don't relate to each other." All Lomax could say in response was "huh."

"Now, sir, on another note, hear me out before you start objecting. I contacted Dr. Feldman and discussed the progress of my healing with her. I have an appointment with her tomorrow morning when, hopefully, she will sign off on my early return to modified duty." She waited for Lomax to explode.

"Then when are you going to get here? You have a lot of work to do. Also, as expected, Israel has sent two replacement agents who have been cleared by the state department. I have no doubt that they are also Mossad. I just wanted to give you a heads up."

After getting off the phone with the SAC, she called Darcy. "Hi, Jeannie. You are probably sick of being asked how you feel, but how do you feel?"

"I feel great. In fact, the doctor has given me clearance to return to work so I will be in tomorrow morning. *Just a little fib.* Can you do me a favor? I was going to ask Sandy to call all the team members for a briefing tomorrow at 11 a.m., but Lomax told me she's out today with a sick kid. Can you and Burk notify everyone? There is a big break in the case. Oh, and there are two new Mossad agents who should also be notified."

She stopped at the hospital to check in on Ismail before going to the bureau.

"God, I've heard of a lot of excuses for not going to work, but this takes the cake," Jeannie said as she entered Ismail's hospital room. She was carrying in several helium filled balloons with the words "Get Well Soon" and a box of candy. His wife was at his side and walked to Jeannie and gave her a hug. "So, how is he doing?"

"He's crabby and wants to go home."

"Hey, you know, I can hear you two. What about me? I was the one who was shot. Can a guy get some sympathy here?"

You got it, Ace. I will call the head nurse you despise so much and have her change out your catheter."

"Very funny."

"Poor baby, and if you remember, I got shot also."

"You only got a scratch. Me, if it wasn't for being in such excellent shape and quick like a cat on my feet, I might be up there (pointing to heaven)." Both Jeannie and Ismail's wife began to laugh.

"I checked with the doctor, and she said you get to go home in a few more days. She wants you to rehab for at least a month before entertaining a return to duty. Before you say anything, the SAC agrees and said you are not allowed in the building until that time."

"Yeah, yeah, I heard. I don't know how you are going to be able to solve any cases without me, though. Maybe you should check in with me every few hours and I can direct you in your cases. You know, like your personal consultant."

Jeannie looked at Ismail's wife. "I'm going to ask the doctor to order a complete psychological exam while he is in rehab."

"I can still hear you."

Jeannie found Lomax at his desk. "Welcome back. I'm not going to ask how you are feeling. I stopped by and saw Flores this morning. He, too, can't wait to get back to work, but his doctor told me he is having problems with controlling his left leg. He is hoping that physical therapy will resolve the issue, but it might be permanent." Jeannie felt tears forming in her eyes.

Lomax got notified that Mossad Agents Lieberman and Alderman were at the front desk. "Okay, check their credentials and then issue them their visitor badges, and then buzz them through. Oh, and get someone to escort them to the breakroom on this floor." Turning to Jeannie, he gave her the names of the two agents and together, they walked down the hallway.

They met them halfway to the briefing room. "Hello, my name is Joseph Alderman, and this is Eleazar Lieberman."

Lomax introduced himself along with Jeannie. They entered the breakroom and were offered coffee or tea. “How are Ariel and Levi doing?” Jeannie asked.

“They are doing well,” Lieberman answered. “Ariel will be back at work soon, but Levi will have to undergo a second surgery on his broken leg.” Lomax had arranged for a catering company to set up breakfast in the largest briefing room. Jeannie remembered how Ismail, upon learning a catering firm was coming to make breakfast, would bring linguicia for them to prepare for him. She caught herself smiling. She turned her attention back to the two agents.

Liebermann appeared and acted like the senior of the two. His beard and mustache were cut extremely close to his face. It appeared that he wore bi-focals. He was tall and thin yet had an air of confidence about him. He wore a black pullover sweater and matching pants.

His partner was a little shorter but much stockier and was dressed a little more casually in a blue golf shirt, tan dockers, and matching slip-ons.

The room filled quickly as the aroma of breakfast invaded the building. Jeannie was quickly tiring of all the welcome backs and how do you feel conversations. She introduced Lieberman and Alderman to a few of her agents and grabbed breakfast before turning her attention to the large smartboard at the front of the room. She connected her laptop to the side of the smartboard and turned on her computer. The first picture displayed was a front shot of the residence on Grand Street. After everyone finished breakfast and the catering crew finished cleaning up and left, Jeannie started the meeting.

"First, I want to thank everyone for your warm concerns about my health and that of Ismail. Before I begin, I would like to hold a moment of silence for our fallen co-workers. They will be missed." Silence filled the room. Jeannie waited a full minute before reconvening.

"I would like to introduce two new agents from Israel who will be working with us. For those of you who do not know, they will replace Agents Segal and Cohen who were both injured in the shootout a few weeks ago. I have been informed that both are on the road to recovery." Everyone in the room clapped. Aldermann nodded while Lieberman raised his hand as if to wave.

"Where to begin?" Jeannie asked. "Perhaps I will start from the aftermath of the shootout. The suspects were looking specifically for maps and Detwrick's diary. In our search of his residence, we found a hidden room (slide showed the door leading to the room and the interior). As you can see, this room contained Nazi gold bars, a large amount of currency, jewelry, paintings and other valuables, plus SS items of value to Detwrick.

"Marsha and her team had started to log and pack items to be moved here (slide showing the room before the gunmen entered). That's when all hell broke loose. After the shooting, they took only one cardboard box, the one labeled 'maps and diary' by Marsha. They left gold and other valuables on the floor and in the room.

"Unknown to the suspects, Marsha had only put the maps in the box, and not this (slide showing the diary)." Jeannie noticed both Mossad agents leaning forward in their chairs. "We do not know what details are on the maps. We can speculate that it shows the location of the gold train."

"Excuse me, Jeannie. I'm new to the team. What gold train are you referring to?"

"Not a problem. In fact, I apologize, since I see several new faces while I have been out. Please come up and introduce yourself later. Now, where was I?"

"Sorry, Jeannie. I have an announcement first," said Lomax. Jeannie had noticed that he seemed to be acting a little crafty today, constantly establishing eye contact with Darcy, Burk, and her secretary. *I hope it is not a damn welcome back cake, she thought.*

The door to the briefing room opened and there, in a wheelchair, was Ismail, being pushed into the room by his wife. Everyone stood and began to clap. "You can't keep a tough guy down," Ismail shouted with the largest smile Jeannie had ever seen him display. His wife was crying and went up to Jeannie and gave her a hug. Jeannie also started to cry. She gave Ismail a big hug and kissed the top of his bald head. Ismail was in his glory.

As the noise level began to return to normal, Lomax once again took over the floor. "It has also come to my attention that today is someone's birthday." On cue, the original catering firm re-entered the room pushing a cart with a multi-level birthday cake.

"We wanted them to light the candles, but there would be too many and it would set off the sprinkler system," Ismail said. Everyone laughed. Jeannie's tears continue to fall. Ismail started it off and everyone sang happy birthday to Jeannie. *Shit, I forgot it's my birthday.*

Ismail again, "Speech, Speech!" All eyes turned to Jeannie.

"Gee, I …. I don't know what to say. My little buddy's back," looking at Ismail. That's the best birthday present ever, and I am glad that you didn't put a whole bunch of candles on the cake since I am forty and holding." More laughter. She wiped the tears from her cheek. "Well, there goes the masacra. Let's eat some cake, and then I will start up again."

30

CHAPTER

WITH EVERYONE NOW stuffed with cake, soda, or coffee, Jeannie once again took the floor. Ismail's wife said her goodbyes, saying she would return in a few hours and to make sure Ismail did not get out of his chair and bug the hell out of everyone. Jeannie guaranteed her request.

"For some of you, this may sound repetitive, but since, as you can see, our mini task force has grown, I feel a review is necessary."

She turned her computer back on. She looked at the new agent and repeated his question before answering, "We are talking about a phantom gold train, loaded with stolen Jewish valuables, ordered by Adolf Hitler to be hidden in a tunnel. The funds from the stolen treasure were to ensure the rise of a new Fourth Reich. You will learn more as I go along." The agent nodded his thanks.

"Nazi plunder, *Raubkunst* in German *(had to show off my ability to speak German),* was the theft of art and other items as a result of the organized looting of European countries during the time of the Nazi Party in Germany. The looting of Polish and Jewish property was a key part of the Holocaust. The plundering was carried out from 1933, beginning with the seizure of German Jews' property, until the end of

World War II, particularly by military units known as the Kunstschutz, although most of the plunder was acquired during the war. In addition to gold, silver, and currency, cultural items of great significance were stolen, including paintings, ceramics, books, and religious treasures.

"Although most of these items were recovered by agents of the Monuments, Fine Art, and Archives program, the *Monument Men,* if you have seen the movie, on behalf of the Allies immediately following the war, many of them are still missing.

"With the implementation of the final solution, the complete elimination of all European Jews, the systematic dispossession of Jewish people and the transfer of their homes, businesses, artworks, financial assets, musical instruments, books, and even home furnishings to the Reich were integral components of the Holocaust. In every country controlled by Nazis, Jews were stripped of their assets through a wide array of mechanisms and Nazi looting organizations.

"In 1940, Hermann Goering, Hitler's number two, issued an order that effectively mandated the seizure of all "Jewish" art collections and other objects of value for the Third Reich. Goering also commanded that the loot would first be divided between Hitler and himself. Hitler later ordered that all confiscated works of art were to be made directly available to him."

Jeannie could not see who shouted out, "Greedy bastard, huh?" but she shared this sentiment. "So, what was all this ill-gained wealth for, you might be asking yourself? After Hitler became chancellor, he made plans to transform his home city Linz, Austria, into the Third Reich's capital city for the arts. Hitler hired architects to work from his own designs to build several galleries and museums, which would collectively be known as the Führermuseum (slide advance). Here is what it was supposed to look like.

"Hitler wanted to fill his museum with the greatest art treasures in the world and believed that most of the world's finest art belonged to Germany after having been looted during the Napoleonic and First World wars.

"The Third Reich amassed hundreds of thousands of objects from occupied nations and stored them in several key locations, including in Paris and the Nazi headquarters in Munich. But the war was shifting against Hitler and his 1,000-year Reich. As the Allied forces gained the advantage in the war and began bombing Germany's cities and historic institutions, Germany began storing the artworks in salt mines and caves for protection from Allied bombing raids.

"These mines and caves offered the appropriate humidity and temperature conditions for artworks. The mines were not only used for the storage of looted art but also for art that had been in Germany and Austria before the beginning of Nazi rule.

"But it was not just artwork that the Nazis seized. In their concentration and death camps, victims had to strip completely before their murder, and all their personal belongings were stolen. These very valuable items, like gold coins, rings, spectacles, jewelry, and other precious metal items, were sent to the Reichsbank, the Nazis' bank, for conversion to bullion. The value was then credited to SS accounts." Jeannie stopped for another gulp of coffee.

Another new and younger agent raised her hand. "Agent Loomis, I think my husband and I saw a documentary or something on the television a few months ago about Hitler's gold train being discovered in a tunnel or cave. Is this related to our case?"

Jeannie smiled and noticed that a lot of the younger agents had been mystified by her background information. "Yes, you are correct. Treasure hunters have been searching for hidden caves, mines, and tunnels for missing Nazi loot since the end of the war. Most of these searches are being conducted based on rumors of Hitler ordering his treasures be hidden so that in the event the Third Reich lost the war, a future generation could create a new Fourth Reich, as I've explained.

"The biggest headline grabber was back in 2016 or 2017 when two amateur treasure hunters said they had 'irrefutable proof' of the existence of a World War II-era Nazi train, rumored to be filled with stolen gold. They claimed that by using ground-penetrating radar to locate the train, they had found railroad tracks in southwestern Poland. However, after analyzing mining data, Polish experts said there was no evidence of the buried train.

"I think this gives everyone a good review of whether or not a phantom gold train exists and the environment that existed that might have warranted hiding such a train. Now, back to our investigation.

"Now, this slide is a close-up of the diary found in Detwrick's secret room. Franz Detwrick was an officer in the Waffen SS. After initial training in Dachau, where he learned how to mistreat Hitler's undesirables, he was sent to several other camps before he landed here; one of the most notorious new extermination camps, Sobibor (slide advance showing the layout of Sobibor as it appeared when it first opened and again in the summer of 1943).

"As you can see from this slide, the railroad track stopped outside the camp. After several unsuccessful escape attempts by the human cargo transported to the death camp, Detwrick came up with the idea to change the path of the train tracks and re-route them, as you can see it this slide. A train would now enter the camp here (pointing using a laser pointer), and this newly installed gate would then be closed before the transport doors were opened. Again, this track was an extension of the original line and was all designed by Detwrick. It was an effective measure to eliminate possible escapes of the human cargo arriving almost daily.

"Detwrick received accolades from Henrick Himmler, head of the SS, and was transferred to various extermination camps to evaluate their railroad systems. His work also caught the eye of Herman Goering, Hitler's second in command."

Jeannie took another sip of coffee and winked at Ismail. "In his diary, Detwrick wrote about the vast wealth the Nazis had accumulated from the Jews and various museums in their occupied territories. I know I am getting old, but I remember learning about the Holocaust in high school and later in college. Can I get a show of hands regarding how many of you know the history of the final solution?

Only half the agents present raised their hands. *God help us, Jeannie thought. And these individuals have the same power to vote as I do.* Some of those that did not raise their hand appeared embarrassed by the fact.

"Okay. That's alright. Just shows you how great our education system in the United States has become," Jeannie said. "But that discussion is for another day.

"Let me give you another short history lesson, and I encourage our SAC to jump in with anything he wishes since his knowledge is greater than mine. Right after Adolf Hitler became chancellor of Germany, his political party, the Nazis, began rounding up individuals they deemed undesirable. Initially, these were communists and political prisoners who despised the Nazis and their ideology.

"But this quickly expanded into the genocide of European Jews during World War II. Between 1941 and 1945, Nazi Germany and its collaborators systematically murdered some six million Jews across German-occupied Europe; around two-thirds of Europe's Jewish population." Jeannie noticed one of the new female agents make the sign of the cross.

"The murders were carried out in what were called pogroms and mass shootings, by a policy of extermination through hard labor in concentration camps, and in gas chambers and gas vans in German extermination camps, chiefly in Auschwitz-Birkenau, Belsec, Chelmno, Majdanek, Treblinka and Sobibor, all located in occupied Poland." She quickly showed slides of the camps after they were liberated, causing the same female agent to excuse herself. No one spoke after the last slide was shown.

"This even included the removal of gold and silver-filled teeth from the Jews after their gassing (slide advance showing a coffee can full of teeth)." Jeannie heard someone say, "Oh, my God." *Had to be one of the newer agents who did not have any history lessons in school.*

"Initially, Goering was placed in charge of transferring the ill-gotten wealth back to Germany to eventually be placed in a yet-to-be-built Fuhrermuseum (slide advance showing drawings of the future site). Its purpose was to display a selection of the art confiscated or stolen by the Nazis from throughout Europe during World War II. The cultural district was part of an overall plan to recreate Linz, Austria, to be the cultural capital of Nazi Germany and one of the greatest art centers in Europe, overshadowing Vienna, for which Hitler had a personal distaste.

"The expected completion date for the project was 1950, but neither the Führermuseum nor the cultural center it was to anchor were built. Why? Because the outcome of the war was going against Germany.

"In August 1942, with the Nazis suffering a defeat in their attack against Russia in Stalingrad, Hitler ordered Goering to start making plans to distribute the wealth taken from the Jewish communities and store it primarily in occupied territories.

"As the outcome of the war became bleaker and bleaker, Hitler gave an order called the Nero Decree.

If you saw the movie *The Monument Men*, you will remember how some art was stored in mines and caves, even tunnels, but the fanatical SS blindly carried out his order to destroy the masterpieces before they fell into the Allies' hands. If the art was not to be displayed in the Führermuseum, it would never be seen again by anyone."

Jeannie stopped and swallowed some more coffee while smiling at Ismail before continuing. "Goering refused to carry out Hitler's orders, as did Albert Speer, his chief architect, who was told to implement a scorched earth policy. Detwrick was ordered to organize the transportation of art to the Führerbunker in Berlin. This was before Hitler sought shelter there, where he had hoped, under his military guidance, the Nazis could retake the offensive. We all know that this did not materialize, and later Hitler killed himself."

"Do we know what happened to the art that was in the bunker?" Lomax asked. "I mean, the Russians were the first to get there, so I assume they hoarded it for themselves."

"Detwrick said as much in his diary. I will tell everyone about his capture near the Führerbunker, but first, back to a secret mission given to Detwrick by Goering. As I think I alluded to, Goering liked what he saw regarding Detwrick's redesigning of railroad lines in Poland. With the war going badly and running out of places to hide the stolen wealth that would be needed to build the Fourth Reich, Goering placed him in charge of building a railroad line off the existing railway located in Linz, Austria, to a not yet dug tunnel in this mountain (slide advance showing Mt. Gamsfeld.)

"As the railroad lines were being laid, by forced labor I should add, Goering kept Detwrick appraised about the future date of the gold train's arrival. Detwrick kept records of the progress made each week on running the new line of track and the dynamiting of a location in the mountain for the tunnel. He was very detailed in his writings, and it was easy to follow, but all that changed when the new railroad line approached the mountain. As I said, he began using code. I can only assume that the code reveals the exact location of the tunnel and everything about its dimensions, plus when the gold train arrived if it did. Okay, let's take a break."

"Pretty snazzy set of wheels there, Ace," Jeannie said when she reached the back of the room where Ismail was seated next to Burk.

"Hey, boss lady. This is only temporary until I get me sea legs back. I know how urgently you need my investigative talent to help you solve this phantom train thing."

"You, mister, need to take care of yourself first. We've got this covered. The further we get into this, the more likely we will be turning the matter over to authorities in Europe. We might even get Interpol involved." Her thoughts turned to Delaney. "So, how is physical therapy going?"

"Rocky is a brutal dude. I mean, he makes me cry. I could see him as an SS officer. Now, Annette, she's a knockout, and after my workout, her massages are to dream for."

"Still a pervert, I see." She got Ismail a second slice of her birthday cake and one for herself and then headed back up front.

"Alright, where was I? Oh, yes, the main focus of the last section of his diary dealt with the construction of the railroad line and tunnel, but, as I said, it's in code. Darcy and Burk will be assigned the decoding of that portion of the diary.

"Now, about his arrest near the Führerbunker in Berlin near the end of the war. He mentioned in his diary that he had gone to the bunker the day after Hitler arrived. Hitler still had delusions of grandeur (she looked at Ismail and smiled), believing that he could command to victory divisions that no longer existed. This would be January 17, 1945. He met with old Adolf to give him an update regarding the hiding of the gold train and its location.

"Now, it is only speculation, but he may have given Hitler copies of the maps, his diary, and keys to the gate and train card, and God knows where they ended up. But it is also possible that he only gave Hitler a copy of the maps and kept the diary. Since he had maps and his diary in his safe, we know he kept the items for himself after the war.

"He talks about how Hitler was a ruined man by this stage of the war. He noted that, when he personally met him in the bunker, Hitler could not hide the trembling of his left hand and arm. He kept assuring Detwrick that a new offensive would turn back the advancing Russians, and then he would push the Allies back to Normandy. Detwrick received a medal from Hitler for what he had accomplished, not only for the Third Reich but also for the future Fourth Reich.

"Later, for some unknown reason, he returned to Berlin, where he was arrested by the Russians. We also don't know why they turned him over to the American Army. Again, who knows? This, like the phantom ghost train, is shrouded in mystery. He may have used the time to hide his stolen treasure or arrange to have funds sent to him later. If he wrote about it in his diary, it is coded."

The same new agent who asked a question earlier raised her hand. "Jeannie, sometimes you mention gold train and sometimes ghost train or phantom train. Are they one and the same?"

"Yes. Both Detwrick and Goering interchanged the name of the train, but Detwrick also mentioned that he was led to believe, after talks with Goering, that there were numerous other ghost trains destined to be placed in tunnels, mines and caves throughout the Nazis' occupied territories. Naturally, Goering never discussed their exact locations. This makes sense if you consider the vast amount of loot seized by the Nazis from the beginning of World War II.

"Okay, with everything I have covered, I have assignments for each team to jump on immediately, which I've given to Burk and Darcy, so see them as you leave. If you have any questions, contact me 24/7."

31

CHAPTER

ELEAZAR LIEBERMAN AND Joseph Alderman asked if they could assist Darcy and Burk in the decoding of the diary. Jeannie anticipated their request and personally introduced them to her highly talented tech team. Darcy had already made copies of the coded sections of the diary and gave them to Lieberman and Joseph. "That's an unusual name, Eleazar?" Darcy said while giving him copies.

"It is an ancient name for one of the chief zealots who held off the Romans from the mountain fortress, Masada. Have you heard of such a place?" Before she could answer, Lomax entered the room after overhearing what Eleazar had said.

"Built by King Herod the Great King of Judea, who originally built Masada as a castle complex in the last century B.C. Recognizing the defensive advantages of Masada, Herod built his complex there as a winter escape and haven from enemies, complete with a castle, storerooms, cisterns, and a foreboding wall. When the Romans overtook Judea in the first century A.D., the grounds became a fortress for the Jewish people.

"Eleazar Ben Yair, from whose name yours was derived, fled from Jerusalem to Masada to command a group of Judean rebels. After several months of siege without success, the Romans built a tower and pulled it up a man-made ramp to try and take out the fortress's wall.

"When it became clear that the Romans were going to take over Masada, on April 15, 73 A.D., on the instructions of Ben Yair, all but two women and five children, who hid in the cisterns and later told their stories, took their own lives rather than live as Roman slaves. How'd I do?" Lomax asked.

"You've impressed me," Burk said.

"Me, too," said Darcy.

"Your knowledge of ancient Israel is indeed very impressive, Agent Lomax, Lieberman said. "Have you been there?"

"No, but it is on my bucket list," he replied, remembering a similar conversation with the first two Mossad agents. "Can you get me a copy of the coded section of the diary, Darcy?" he asked.

After giving Lomax a copy of the coded sections, she and Burk cleared two desks for their guests. She then pulled two ceramic coffee cups from her desk drawer and handed them to the agents. "You already know where the coffee room is, so help yourself."

Jeannie made her way around the office, checking in on the progress of her various teams. One of the new agents who had asked questions at the meeting introduced himself. Randy Carter was a recent graduate from Quantico. She guessed he was around twenty-five years old and nice looking. He had thick sandy colored hair and green eyes. He was clean-shaven, and it appeared that he had nicked himself while shaving this morning. *God, did I look this young when I started with the bureau?* She welcomed him onboard.

As she started walking away, he quickly followed her. "Agent Loomis, would it be possible to work on the coded sections of the diary? I took a course in cryptology at Quantico, and I might be able to help if that's okay?"

"Call me Jeannie. That might not be a bad idea since you probably were taught new techniques that Darcy and Burk may not know about. Report to them first thing in the morning."

She ended with a visit to Burk, Darcy, and the two new Mossad agents. "Got it solved yet?" she asked, teasing.

"Agent Loomis," said Alderman. "Will we be allowed to take these copies to our hotel room?"

"First, call me Jeannie. Let me check with my supervisor, but I don't think that will be a problem. She looked at Burk and Darcy. "One of our new agents, Randy Carter, will be joining your group tomorrow morning. He took cryptology courses recently in Quantico and offered his assistance."

She then walked down the hallway to the SAC's office, where she found Lomax putting on his jacket and getting ready to leave.

"I'm leaving early today. I got copies of the coded sections of the diary and want to do some work from home. Happy birthday, by the way."

"I know you were behind both the visit from Ismail and the birthday cake. I can't thank you enough. Our two new Mossad agents want permission to take their copies of the coded messages to their hotel room. I said I would check with you."

Lomax thought about it. "They will take them back to their hotel rooms, but you know they will quickly be sent to Israel." He paused. "Go ahead and let them take them. I had a good meeting with their boss, a Mr. Goldman, who is high up in Mossad, by the way. I don't think they are going to screw us. Besides, after you called me last night about the possible location in Austria, I called our international office and told them to report any increase in activity near Linz."

***

Once home, Lomax greeted his wife, who had an early dinner waiting for him. "Interesting day?" she asked, giving him a kiss. "I made pork chops, dressing, and cream corn for dinner." The kitchen table was already laid with dishes and cups. As Lomax took his seat, she began serving.

"It was a very interesting day. There may be an actual ghost train belonging to the Nazis. I hope you don't mind, but once I finish dinner and help with the dishes, I want to do some work in my den."

"You don't need to do the dishes. Eat up and get back to work," she said, kissing him on the crown of his head as she placed two pork chops on his plate.

***

Five o'clock came, and all four agents were still working in Darcy and Burk's office. "Hey guys, it's quitting time." Looking at the two Mossad agents, Jeannie told them that they were clear to take copies of the diary to their hotel. "See everyone in the morning, and thanks for all the hard work."

Solving puzzles had never been one of Jeannie's strong suits. She tried not to get frustrated with the damn commute home. It was nice being back in her expensive sports car going a whopping 15 mph. Finally arriving at the bridge, she exhaled, *almost home.* She rolled down the window of the Corvette. The wind was really blowing, so the scent of the bay waters overcame the exhaust fumes. She cranked up the volume of John Williams, *Dry Your Eyes Africa*, hitting replay four times.

She parked her car in the garage and entered her home. *No Delores. The coast was clear.* "Did you guys miss me?" she asked as her koi raced to the top of their aquarium, waiting for their food pellets. "Boy, you guys are hungry. How was my day, you asked? Well, let me get changed and get some dinner ready, and I will tell you."

32

CHAPTER

LOMAX SLID OPEN one half of his closet door and removed one of his prized positions from a shelf. A genuine World War II German Enigma machine, a cipher device developed and used in the early to mid-20th century to protect commercial, diplomatic, and military communication. It was employed extensively by Nazi Germany during World War II in all branches of the German military. *Perhaps Detwrick used a device similar to this. Can't hurt trying.*

The Enigma has an electromechanical rotor mechanism that scrambles the 26 letters of the alphabet. In typical use, one person enters text on the Enigma's keyboard, and another person writes down which of the 26 lights above the keyboard illuminates at each key press. If plain text is entered, the illuminated letters are the encoded ciphertext. Entering the ciphertext transforms it back into readable plaintext. The rotor mechanism changes the electrical connections between the keys and the lights with each key press. Lomax began entering each German letter making up the code into the Enigma.

***

"Good evening, Sir, Lieberman said once Goldman answered his phone. "Yes, Lomax gave us permission to bring the codes to our hotel room. We will scan and send them immediately. There are four of us working on this part of the investigation. Two FBI agents who are very good with computers and Joseph and me. A new agent will join our group tomorrow. All we know about him is that he just completed training in the FBI training center and has the latest knowledge about breaking codes. Our first few attempts of decoding today were fruitless. We are to meet in the morning and try again. If our agency cracks it, will we be sharing with the Americans?"

"That has not been determined yet. I will be expecting your email with the coded sections."

***

Jeannie finished her dinner and took a piece of her leftover birthday cake. She carried it upstairs to her bedroom, where pictures of Detwrick and the Hetmans were displayed on a wall. "This needs to be updated." She downloaded the pictures from Detwrick's hidden room before the shootout and added them to the wall. In the process, her phone rang. It was Ismail.

"Hey, boss lady, feel any older?" he said, laughing.

"Forty and holding."

"Yeah, right. So, did you guys make any progress today?" Jeannie brought him up to speed. "Wish I could be there to add my expert solving skills."

"Wish you were there also, buddy, but you have to get well." She told him how Detwrick switched over to an unknown code, like gibberish, when he got closer to revealing details of the tunnel and train. Ismail asked if he could get a copy and work on it since he was bored out of his mind. Jeannie said she would have Darcy send him an email attachment. "I will call you tomorrow evening and give you another update."

"Alright, but if I don't hear from you, I will call. When you get old, you start getting forgetful." With that, Ismail hung up. *Little shit.* She returned to the wall and stared at the new material. She started rubbing her forehead. *Nothing. It all hinges on decoding that damn diary.*

She got up very early the next morning, unable to sleep soundly due to the excitement of the chase. She made scrambled eggs and linguiça while thinking of Ismail. She had prayed like never before that he would not die while he was in his coma. Now, she prayed for his full recovery. *Another cup of coffee, and it's time to hit the road.* She fed her fish and told them goodbye.

Beating most of the commuter traffic, she stopped at a local donut and bagel shop and picked up munchies for her team.

Instead of going directly to the office, she first made a detour to the house on Grand Street. The crime scene tape had been removed and replaced by a building department notice saying that the house was unsafe to enter. She remained in her car eating a bagel, hoping that looking at the house would give her some new inspiration or insight on how to progress, or, at least, on what she had overlooked. Her thoughts then turned to the shooting, and she quickly started her car and left.

She was surprised to see Lomax's car already there when she drove into the parking lot. After placing the food in the breakroom, she made her way to his office. "Boy, you're here early. I picked up some donuts and bagels, if you want to join me?"

"That sounds like it would hit the spot," he said as he got up and walked with her down the hall. "I tried to work on the coded portion of the diary last night, but my idea didn't work out."

"What idea was that?"

"As you know, I love history, and I have quite a collection of World War I and II artifacts at home. Have you ever heard of the Enigma?"

"Enigma? No, can't recall ever hearing the name."

"The Enigma machine was a famous encryption machine used by the Germans during WWII to transmit coded messages. It allowed for billions and billions of ways to encode a message, making it incredibly difficult for other nations to crack German codes during the war; for a time, the code seemed unbreakable."

"The Royal Navy captured a German U-boat in the North Atlantic in 1941 and recovered their Enigma machine, its cipher keys, and the code books that allowed codebreakers to read German signal traffic during World War II. I have a genuine Enigma machine in my house."

"Wow. You really are a history nut."

Lomax laughed. "I tried all night to see if the machine could help break Detwrick's code, but I was unsuccessful. Hopefully, Darcy and Burk will have better luck."

"I thought of something as I drove home last night after you gave permission for our Mossad agents to take copies of the coded messages to their hotel room. If we break the code, are we going to share it?"

Lomax looked at Jeannie. "I think we must. I only hope that if Israel breaks it, they too will share."

Burk and Darcy arrived in the breakroom next. Both made green tea. Jeannie thought of Ismail, who saw them making tea one day and called them Millennials. "Good morning, everyone," a bright and cheerful Darcy said.

"Why are you so chipper this morning? Did you two solve the code?" Lomax asked.

Burk, who was still intimidated by Lomax, stood and quickly replied, "No, Sir. Not yet, but we are on it." Jeannie looked at Lomax, who winked at her. Soon, the two Mossad agents arrived and helped themselves to food and coffee. Lomax excused himself after filling up his cup and taking another donut. The last to arrive was Agent Carter. Jeannie introduced him to the rest of the team and left. She then turned and re-entered the room.

"The SAC thought that maybe the code was somehow related to the Germans' Enigma machine. He has an authentic working machine at his home. You won't need to go down that avenue, though, since it did not work at decoding the diary. Darcy, can I see you a minute?"

Down the hallway, away from the breakroom, Jeannie asked Darcy to cover her tracks if she and Burk decided to use "outside" sources to help decipher the code. "I just want to make sure that our two Israeli agents don't learn all our secrets." Darcy understood and would pass it on to Burk in private.

Four days passed, and still no breakthrough. Unbeknown to the two Mossad agents, and even Agent Carter, Darcy had used her contacts at the CIA, who also had been unsuccessful. Sensing frustration setting in, Jeannie had a few pizzas and drinks delivered directly to Darcy and Burk's office.

She joked and teased them while eating; anything to get their minds off the puzzlement of the code.

Jeannie looked at Carter. "In Quantico, did they ever discuss how to proceed when faced with what appears to be an unbreakable code?"

"Actually, I was just thinking about that. As we all know, the opposite of enciphering and encoding is deciphering and decoding. I know this is basic but hear me out. In other words, ciphers are different from code. When you substitute one word for another word or sentence, like using a foreign language dictionary, you are using a code. When you mix up or substitute existing letters, you are using a cipher. For a cipher to be useful, several things must be known at both the sending and receiving ends."

"Therefore, three things are needed. One, we must know the algorithm or method used to encipher. Two, we need to know the key used with the algorithm to allow the plaintext to be both enciphered and deciphered. And finally, number three, we must know the period during which the key is valid."

"Okay, impressive, but you're starting to go over my head," Jeannie said.

"Look at it this way, Jeannie. When you go home and enter your house through a locked door, you put your key into the lock, and it opens. The process, the key into the lock, is the algorithm. Now, this only works when you put the proper key into the proper lock."

"Alright, so far, so good. Go ahead."

"Your key should not open your neighbor's lock. Why? Because the algorithm is different. The selection of those three elements, algorithm, key, and period/ time, depends on your needs."

"If you are on a battlefield and are receiving current tactical data, you want an algorithm that makes it easier to decipher the message in the heat of battle. This does not apply to Detwrick."

"On the other hand, you must also assume that your opponent has intercepted your enciphered message and is busy trying to break it. The easier the algorithm you choose, the more often you will have to change the key that unlocks the code."

"Substitution ciphers replace letters in the plaintext with other letters or symbols, keeping the order in which the symbols fall the same."

"Transposition ciphers keep all the original letters intact but mix up their order. Of course, Detwrick could have used both methods one after the other to further confuse someone trying to break the code, like us."

"With this basic knowledge in mind, we must decide, under the circumstances Detwrick found himself, would it be best to use substitution ciphers or transposition ciphers."

"Hey, Jeannie, where did you get this guy? Wow," said Darcy

33

CHAPTER

JEANNIE CAME HOME mentally exhausted. The lecture by Carter was at first, hard to follow, but afterward, she felt that they might never solve Detwrick's code. There seemed to be so many variables involved. Her phone rang. It was Lomax. "Any progress today? I had to leave early for a dentist appointment, and I swung by Flores' house. He said hi, by the way."

"How's he doing?"

"When his wife walked me to the door, she told me that he is not having much improvement in the use of his leg. He's depressed and refuses to take the meds the doctor gave him. Maybe when you get time, you can stop by and encourage or something."

"I'll stop by in the morning on my way in. Back to your question; even with the help of our friends at Langley, we still have not broken the code. I don't feel that our Mossad agents are getting any help from

Israel, either. Our new agent, Randy Carter, really put on a show about cryptology. Have you met him yet?"

"No, I saw his file when he arrived, but because of all the excitement, I have not held my orientation meeting with him yet. He's working on decoding the diary?"

"Yes, he came to me and asked if he could be assigned to that team since he took a cryptology course at Quantico. He really knows his stuff, but it didn't help solve the mystery.

I'm going to take a hot shower and read Detwrick's journal again. Maybe I missed something that might help."

"Okay, see you in the morning."

Jeannie made what her dad used to call a wet sandwich. The only safe place to eat it was over the sink. She got a quarter-length piece of French bread and cut it in half, then placed it in the microwave for twenty seconds to get it toasty. She added a thick layer of mayonnaise, horseradish sauce, Dijon mustard, a layer of Swiss cheese, red onion, Greek pepperoncini peppers, sprouts, a layer of deli turkey, roast beef, ham, tomatoes, sprouts, and cut slices of green bell pepper. *That should do it.* She pushed down on the sandwich and cut it in half. She placed it on a dish and slid it over to the sink. From the top of her refrigerator, she grabbed a bag of Dorito chips, opened the refrigerator again, and took out a can of diet Coke. *Dad would be proud.*

As predicted, juices and part of the makings of the sandwich fell into the sink, but boy, was it good. Using a roll of paper towels, she wiped her face and laid the plate in the sink. She made a cup of coffee and went upstairs, turning on the water in her bathtub. She poured in some bubble bath and took off her clothes while the tub filled. When it was ready, she climbed in and laid back with her head on the back of the tub. She got her washcloth, got it wet, and placed it on her forehead. The stitches had been removed, but she had not yet seen a plastic surgeon about the scar on her forehead. *Something to talk about over cocktails. Now think, Jeannie, think.*

***

Lomax was doing the same thing without the bubble bath. Detwrick was a very organized and detail-oriented individual. He prided himself on being a stormtrooper and appeared to enjoy watching men, women, and children go to their deaths. Three-quarters of his diary entries pertained to his time in the camps. He never used code in those sections. It wasn't until he was given the railroad and gold train assignment that he reverted to code. Why?

Was he working with someone else and feared he might inadvertently give up top-secret information if his diary was found, or was it the fact that he was stealing his fair share, an offense that would lead to his immediate execution? Maybe he created it out of fear of Sgt. Meyer discovering it, or other people working on the project.

Or could it be that he feared someone finding it after the war and discovering the location of the train, the train that contained the riches to start the Fourth Reich? Maybe it was a combination of these.

***

Still hungry, *probably due to an adrenaline rush,* Jeannie had a bowl of instant oatmeal after her bubble bath and climbed into bed, turning on her television. After a few moments of channel-surfing, she found a movie that she had watched a long time ago with her dad. The movie, *Hanoi Hilton*, was released in 1987. It was a Vietnam War film that focused on the experiences of American POWs who were held in the infamous Hoa Lo Prison in Hanoi during the 1960s and 1970s, with the story being told from their perspectives. The POWs gave the place the name 'Hanoi Hilton.' The film used fictional characters instead of the names of former POWs.

It focused on the suffering, torture, and brutal treatment the POWs had to deal with daily from their North Vietnamese guards. From the beginning, they had to endure miserable conditions, including poor food and unsanitary conditions. American pilots were the primary POWs sent to the prison. Most were already in poor condition by the time they were captured, injured either during their ejection or in landing on the ground. The guards employed torture methods, like rope bindings, irons, beatings, and prolonged solitary confinement.

The film showed how the POWs resisted the intimidation factor of their tormentors and the strong bonds that developed between them. It was amazing how they developed their own way of communicating without the discovery of the guards. Jeannie remembered that she did a Google search on the infamous prison and learned about their now famous "tap code."

An Air Force Captain, Carlyle S. "Smitty" Harris, was shot down and captured and became a prisoner of the North Vietnamese for eight years. Besides focusing on his pregnant wife and two children back home at the Air Force base in Okinawa, Japan, Harris also wondered how the POWs would be able to maintain any semblance of leadership and morale without a way to communicate with each other.

Shortly after his capture, Harris was placed in a cell in the Hoa Lo Prison, where he remained for the next 2,871 days with four other POWs, and he remembered a conversation with an instructor at his survival school training. The instructor had told him about a tap code that Royal Air Force POWs had used during World War II, and Harris began teaching the other four POWs the code. Their captors put them back in solitary confinement a few days later, but that only helped them spread the code across the seven-cell area and, ultimately, to POWs throughout North Vietnam.

As the war continued and POWs were moved to other camps away from Hanoi, someone always took the tap code with them and was able to pass it on. No matter where you went in the POW system in North Vietnam, if you heard a tap, the guy on the other side of the wall would respond with two knocks in return, and you started the communication process.

Wish their code would help us crack Detwrick's.

The next morning, on her way to the bureau, she stopped in to check on Ismail. "Dr. Loomis here. How is my favorite patient?" she asked when she saw him. He looked tired and haggard and in bad need of a shave. He looked at her but dropped his head uncharacteristically and did not have a smile or smirk on his face. *Uh oh, something's wrong.*

Finally, Ismail looked up at Jeannie but did not offer his usual comebacks. Instead, he yelled at his wife to bring him his breakfast and coffee. "Guy almost dies from getting shot, and his old lady tries to starve him to death. Why are you here? Need my help already? Sorry, I'm a cripple, and you're on your own."

Wow, Jeannie thought. Her partner and friend was going downhill mentally. "Are you through?" she asked tartly. Her comment seemed to have the desired effect on him. "Yes, you were almost killed, and by the grace of God, you survived. Do you know the effect that had on your poor wife and family, not to mention your friends and co-workers? Poor baby. Ismail got shot. Marsha and her team were not that lucky. Neither were the four security guards. Have you given it any thought as to why God allowed you to live?" She let her comments hang in the air.

"Now, listen to me. Your doctor gave you some meds to get over this self-pity you are going through. Where's the highly trained FBI agent everyone admired?" She saw a smile start to form on his face. "Now, take the damn meds, and push yourself at physical therapy. I need you back at the bureau. Hell, if you were there, we would probably already have this God damn case solved. And, God damn it, give your wife a break." Her tirade hung in the air for a few seconds.

Ismail sat up in his chair. "You're right. Without my extraordinary deductive skills, you are not as effective." He started to cry. His wife raced to his side. "Mi amor, you will be okay. You are a good man, and, as Jeannie said, God wants you here with us. You just need to take your medicine and give it time." Jeannie let herself out while the two continued to embrace.

When she got into her car, she cried like the day her fiancé was killed.

34

CHAPTER

JEANNIE FOUND EVERYONE hard at work discussing possible new avenues for attacking the code. Agent Carter was still dazzling everyone with his knowledge of cryptology, but they were no closer to solving the mystery than the day before. Lomax entered the room and told them what he had attempted to do using his Enigma machine. He saw a list of frequently used code systems on a whiteboard. Some he recognized or had heard about, some not. A line had been drawn through most of them, indicating that they were not the code used by Dietwrick.

Carter introduced himself to Lomax, who apologized for not yet holding an orientation meeting with the young agent. As that conversation ended, no one spoke. Jeannie decided to break the silence by discussing the Hanoi Hilton film she watched last night. Other than Lomax, no one else had seen the film nor heard of the infamous prison.

"I saw an interview on the History Channel, a documentary where the survivors, the POWs, were interviewed. Those guys went through hell. They all agreed that what helped them keep their sanity was being able to talk to the other captives by using their code system," Lomax said.

"That follows what you were talking about yesterday, Randy," Jeannie said. Carter looked at her. "You know, the three elements; algorithm, key, and period/time, depending on your needs. In the film, after one of the POWs developed the coding system and everyone learned how to use it, their morale increased dramatically. How that bit of information will help us, I don't know, but I hate it when people are together in a room, and no one speaks." Everyone laughed in agreement. "I'm sure Detwrick did not use a taping code in his diary."

Lomax stood and started walking towards the door, so Jeannie assumed he was leaving the room. Instead, he stopped near the whiteboard and picked up a marker. With his back to the group, he wrote Detwrick. He then turned and faced the room. "Last night, while I was playing with my Enigma machine, I kept remembering some of the things you said about him, Jeannie." Under Detwrick, Lomax wrote several words under each other.

Detwrick

1. SS Officer
2. Loner
3. Death Camps
4. Attention to Detail

"This piece of work (pointing to Detwrick's name) loved being in the Waffen SS. Like most psychopaths, he worked with others to accomplish a task but preferred being alone. Most of his career was spent at various extermination camps, where he observed and made recommendations about camp improvements, mostly railroad lines." Jeannie started to interrupt Lomax but decided to hear him out. "When he was not working on railroad issues, what did he do?"

"The sick bastard, pardon my French, probably supervised the gassing of the poor Jews," Darcy said.

"Exactly. But, more importantly, he used his unique observation skill. His attention, his sharp attention to detail, would be focused on the daily routines of the camps he was assigned. What if, and it's a big what if, he somehow devised his coding system along the lines of the standard operating systems of the death camps, or how the victims tried to communicate with each other like the POWs in the film Jeannie talked about, *Hanoi Hilton*?"

"You might be on to something. We don't have any other avenues right now, do we?" Jeannie asked, looking at everyone in the room. "Alright. Darcy, Burk, come up with a complete list of the camps Detwrick was assigned during the war."

"Jeannie," Lieberman said, "our agency already has that list. If you would like, a phone call to our supervisor, Goldman, will get us those assignments."

"Great, give him a call. Alright, let's take a break, and once Eleazar gets the list, we start focusing on those camps."

Jeannie walked to the restrooms with Lomax. "I hope this develops into something because, frankly, I don't know where else to go."

"You know, I see what you mean about Carter. Pretty sharp cookie, but a little too cocky for my tastes. As you said, the more I talk with him, the more impressed I am with his knowledge of cryptology. Kid might be a rising star."

Fifteen minutes later, everyone was back in the room. Lieberman gave everyone a list of the camps Detwrick had been assigned.

Dachau
Auschwitz - Birkenau
Sobibor
Treblinka
Ravensbruck
Belzec
Mauthausen

Buchenwald
Bergen – Belsen
Sachsenhausen

“Damn, this guy really got around, didn’t he?” Burk said, looking over the list. “How do you want us to handle this?” he asked, looking at Jeannie.

“You five decide. Let’s leave Ravensbruck out for now, so it looks like two apiece since Auschwitz-Birkenau were two sites. Keep me posted on your progress,” Jeannie said as she left.

Carter asked if he could take Sobibor and Treblinka. “Your wish is my command,” Darcy said. “Anyone else?” Lieberman selected Bergen – Belsen and the Sachsenhausen camps. Alderman got Auschwitz-Birkenau, while Burk would focus on Buchenwald and Dachau, leaving Belzec and Mauthausen for Darcy.

Lieberman and Alderman contacted Goldman, asking for their agency to send over all background information on all the camps. “Why work hard when the work has already been done?” Lieberman said. “But be prepared for an avalanche of material.”

Tons of printouts began to arrive from Mossad. “I’ll make sure there is enough paper in the fax machine. This is going to save a lot of time,” Darcy said. “My God, look at the stack just for Mauthausen,” waving the paperwork in her hand. “Alright, I’m going to get a hot tea and hide out in one of the briefing rooms.”

***

Heiliger picked up the phone and began shouting, "Why have you not reported sooner? We are completely in the dark here. Where is the fucking diary? The maps we have are useless. I need answers, damn it. The Organization has many questions."

"Sir, I was just going to call you. The Americans have Detwrick's diary, and an agent has been taking it home to try and decipher it since it is in some unique code. I will text you her address. It is across the bay in a city called Newark. Also, she lives alone.

35

CHAPTER

DARCY REVIEWED HER notes about Mauthausen. She focused her attention on 1941 and beyond since Detwrick was not there prior. She was particularly interested in this camp since Detwrick had mentioned that he thought he was going to be assigned there temporarily until Goering gave him his top-secret job. It was a Nazi concentration camp located on a hill above the market town of Mauthausen, roughly twelve miles east of Linz, in Upper Austria.

It was the main camp of a group of nearly one hundred subcamps located throughout Austria and southern Germany. The inmates at Mauthausen and its subcamps were forced to work as slave labor under conditions that caused many deaths. Mauthausen and its subcamps included quarries, munitions factories, mines, arms factories, and plants assembling fighter aircraft. The conditions at Mauthausen were even more severe than in most other Nazi concentration camps. Half of the 190,000 deportees died at Mauthausen or its subcamps. Mauthausen was one of the first massive concentration camp complexes in Nazi Germany and the last to be liberated by the Allies.

About 200,000 prisoners passed through Mauthausen. Some 120,000 of them died, mainly from starvation, disease, and the hardships of labor. About 38,000 of the dead were Jews.

Mauthausen also had a gas chamber and employed gas vans, and from April 1944 to January 1945, the gas chambers at nearby Hartheim Castle were also used to kill prisoners too weak to work or too "undesirable" to be kept alive. The SS fled Mauthausen shortly before American troops entered the camp on May 5, 1945. *Those cowards.* She found nothing useful for decoding the diary. *Nothing helpful here. Time to take a break.*

Agent Carter felt that if anything were going to be found, it would be in his research of Sobibor. The camp was built by 150 Jewish workers in 1942. Remarkably, the work was completed in just two months. That meant Detwrick arrived shortly after the camp became operational. Also, the camp only existed from May 1942 to October 1943. During that short period, over 250,000 Jews were gassed, mostly coming from Poland and occupied areas of the former Soviet Union. This was during the time Detwrick was assigned there.

The camp was in the forest near the village of Sobibor in occupied Poland. It was an extermination camp rather than a concentration camp and existed for the sole purpose of murdering Jews. Most prisoners were gassed within hours of their arrival.

Those not killed immediately were forced to assist in the operation of the camp, and few survived more than a few months. In total, some 170,000 to 250,000 people were murdered at Sobibor in the short time it was operational, making it the fourth-deadliest Nazi camp after Belzec, Treblinka, and Auschwitz.

On October 14, 1943, some 300 Jewish laborers at the camp rose in revolt and killed several SS supervisors and Ukrainian guards. Many inmates were killed during the rebellion and in their attempts to escape. All who remained were executed the following day. The Nazis dismantled the installations and planted the area with pine trees. Only about fifty Sobibor prisoners ultimately survived the war. *If those who survived did not discuss using a code, it is not here.*

Carter then began reading about the Treblinka camp. There were two camps, but the original, referred to as Treblinka I, was established as a forced labor camp in 1941. In 1942, as part of the final solution, Treblinka II was constructed to be almost purely an extermination center, like Sobibor and Belzec.

The killing center was divided into three parts: the reception area, living area, and killing area. The living area contained housing for the German staff and the guard unit. It also contained administrative offices, a clinic, storerooms, and workshops. One section contained barracks that housed those Jewish prisoners selected from incoming transports to provide forced labor. This forced labor was intended to support the camp's function: mass murder.

My God, Carter said to himself. Over 50-60 cattle cars arrived during each transport. *How many victims were in each transport?* He stopped reading and caught his breath before continuing.

A small number of Jewish men who were not murdered immediately upon arrival became members of its Sonderkommando, whose jobs included being forced to bury the victims' bodies in mass graves. These bodies were exhumed in 1943 and cremated on large open-air pyres, along with the bodies of new victims.

Gassing operations at Treblinka II ended in October 1943 following a revolt by the prisoners in early August. Several Trawniki guards, Central and Eastern European Nazi collaborators, were killed, and over 300 prisoners escaped from the camp; almost 100 survived the subsequent pursuit. The camp was dismantled in late 1943. A farmhouse for a watchman was built on the site, and the ground was plowed over to try and hide the evidence of genocide. Nothing was found about a coding system used. He read more material about the revolt and escape.

On August 2, 1943, prisoners quietly seized weapons from the camp armory. However, they were discovered before they could take over the camp. Hundreds of prisoners stormed the main gate, trying to escape. Many were killed by machinegun fire. More than300 did escape, although two-thirds of them were eventually tracked down and killed by the SS and police. Surviving prisoners were forced to dismantle the camp. *Well, if they used a coding system, it is not discussed in these documents.*

At noon, Jeannie checked in with everyone. The common feedback was questioning how the SS could have been so barbaric in their inhuman treatment of their victims. Some shared stories of the atrocities they read, but the common thread was the lack of any information about codes being found so far. After lunch, they returned to their assigned tasks. Evening came, and still no breakthrough.

36

CHAPTER

BURK SET UP in an empty room down the hall from his shared office with Darcy. He placed the research material pertaining to Buchenwald on a desk and dug in. It was a Nazi concentration camp located on a hill near Weimar, Germany, wherever in the hell that was, he thought. It was one of the first and largest of the concentration camps within Germany's 1937 borders.

Many suspected communists were among the first internees. Prisoners came from all over Europe and the Soviet Union, Jews, Poles, and other Slavs, the mentally ill and physically disabled, political prisoners, Freemasons, and prisoners of war. There were also ordinary criminals and sexual deviants. All prisoners worked primarily as forced labor in local armaments factories. The insufficient food and poor conditions, along with deliberate executions, led to 56,545 deaths of the 280,000 prisoners who passed through Buchenwald and its 139 subcamps. The camp gained notoriety when it was liberated by the

United States Army in April 1945. *No mention of a code system used by inmates. Time to move on.*

Lieberman looked at the stack of papers pertaining to Sachsenhausen. The camp was established in 1936 and was located 35 km north of Berlin, which gave it a primary position among the German concentration camps. It was the administrative center of all concentration camps, and it became a training center for SS officers who would often be sent to oversee other camps once ready. Initially, the camp was used to perfect the most efficient and effective execution method for use in the death camps. Given that, executions obviously took place at Sachsenhausen, especially of Soviet prisoners of war. *Detwrick must have felt right at home there.*

During the earlier stages of the camp's existence, the executions were done by placing the prisoners in a small room, often with music playing, and told they were to have their height and weight measured but were instead shot in the back of the neck through a sliding door located behind them. This was found to be far too time-consuming, so they then marched them to a trench where they killed them either by shooting or hanging.

While this more easily enabled group executions, it created too much initial panic among the prisoners, making them harder to control. Then, small trials of what would go on to become the large-scale gas chambers were designed, and executions were carried out that way. These trials showed the authorities that this method facilitated the means to murder the largest number of prisoners without "excessive" initial panic. So, by September 1941, they were conducting the first trials of this method at Auschwitz. *No mention of inmates using any kind of coding system.*

Lomax took home a list of the death camps compiled by Mossad and being used by Jeannie's team. He was familiar with most of the camps, especially the three most secretive, Sobibor, Treblinka, and Belzec, having visited all three. The ballgame he was watching became a blowout, so he decided to do some research on his computer.

He was not familiar with Ravensbruck and began his Internet search. The Ravensbruck camp was the largest concentration camp for women in the German Reich. It was second only in size to the women's camp in Auschwitz-Birkenau. Construction of the camp began in November 1938 by order of the SS leader, Heinrich Himmler, and was unusual in that it was intended to hold exclusively female inmates.

The SS began construction of the camp in November 1938, located near the village of Ravensbruck in Northern Germany, 80 km from Berlin. The SS authorities transported about 500 male prisoners from Sachsenhausen to build the camp.

The SS required Ravensbruck prisoners to perform forced labor, primarily in agricultural projects and local industry. By 1944, Germany increasingly relied on forced labor to produce armaments. It soon became the administrative center of a system of over forty subcamps with over 70,000 predominantly female prisoners. The greatest number of prisoners at one time in Ravensbrück was probably about 45,000.

There were children in the camp as well. At first, they arrived with Romanian mothers or were born to imprisoned women. Most of these children died of starvation.

Between 1939 and 1945, some 130,000 to 132,000 female prisoners passed through the camp system. Approximately 50,000 women perished from disease, starvation, overwork, and despair. Two thousand two hundred were gassed, according to the Nazis' own records. "Jesus," Lomax said out loud. He was about to finish his research for the night when a citation at the bottom of the articles he was reading caught his eye.

37

CHAPTER

JEANNIE PARKED HER car in the secure lot, noticing that Lomax had once again beaten her in. She checked in with her receptionist who told her that the SAC wanted to see her ASAP. Before she could say anything, Lomax looked up from his desk and asked her where the diary was. Jeannie said she had just locked up again in the evidence locker. They walked together to retrieve it.

"Sounds like you're on a mission," she said.

"Maybe. We shall see." Jeannie signed out for the diary again and gave it to Lomax. "Do you remember reading about him being assigned to Ravensbruck?"

"I don't remember specifically what he said, but I do remember Ravensbruck because when I saw the name, for some reason I thought of Edgar Allan Poe's *The Raven*. Why?"

Lomax did not reply. He turned to the first page where Jeannie had left a yellow paper tab noting where Detwrick had started using his code. He pulled out his phone and called the forensic department, asking for Sid McDonald. Once he got him on the phone, Jeannie heard the order given. She looked at Lomax. "I will explain while we get some coffee and wait for McDonald."

In the breakroom, Lomax told her about a citation he found at the bottom of one of the pages while researching Ravensbruck concentration camp. He said he would tell the whole story to her team if his hunch paid off.

McDonald arrived at the breakroom carrying a clothes iron. Jeannie believed she knew where this was going. Without saying anything, he had McDonald plug in the iron. He folded the diary so that the first page where Detwrick started using code was displayed. After a few minutes, he pressed the hot iron onto the page. "The correct term for what we are seeing is 'letter in moczem,' which means 'letter in urine.'"

There, before their eyes, they saw what Detwrick had done. His writings that looked like German gibberish were just that. Random letters and words used to confuse the reader who would mistake it for code. Instead, written over this gibberish in urine, were his actual entries. Jeannie now had some reading ahead of her.

Her entire team were summoned to a meeting in one hour. Darcy was the first to ask what was so urgent. Jeannie only smiled and said they had a huge break in the case. Lomax ordered Jeannie to head home and reveal what Detwrick had hidden as quickly as possible. She signed out for the diary on the evidence log and headed for home. There would be fewer distractions there than at the bureau. He would address all her team, including Darcy, Burk, Lieberman, Alderman, and Carter, and explain the breakthrough to everyone.

Jeannie was so excited she could not remember the ride home. Once in her house, she located her iron and ironing board. Before plugging it in, she decided to fully charge her cell so she could take pictures of each page as it revealed its secrets. While waiting for the phone to charge, she heated a bowl of soup.

Her phone only being half-charged meant that it was going to take some time. She went upstairs and got her Mac and returned to the kitchen. She found several articles about the women of Ravensbruck.

In 1942, SS leader Heinrich Himmler's personal doctor, a Karl Gebhardt, began using the laboratories at the camp to conduct brutal medical experiments, even calling his victims "rabbits." These tests included treating wounds with various chemical substances to prevent infections. Gebhardt and his team also tested multiple methods of setting and transplanting bones. Such experiments also included amputations.

Eighty women, mostly Polish inmates, were selected and subjected to the Nazis' physicians' horrific experiments. Many died in the process, and those who survived suffered permanent physical and mental damage. However, at that time, such inhumane practices were secret from the outside world and contained inside the walls of the concentration camp.

During these unethical medical examinations, four Polish women were determined to expose the camp's abusive practices against female prisoners to the world. They were Krystyna Czyz, Wanda Wijtaski, Janina Iwaska and her sister, Krystyna Iwaska.

At that time, due to the physical disabilities they suffered in the tests, escaping the camp was impossible. Therefore, they decided to report on the experiments to the Polish resistance, believing it would soon reach the Polish government in exile and foreign governments and might lead to the liberation of their camp. They hoped their reports would also reach the International Red Cross which would inform the world about the horrific crimes being committed by the doctors in the camp.

However, the problem was, how to make that happen? How could they get their reports outside the camp?

Back then, the inmates' only communication method with the outside world was through a letter each inmate was allowed to write to her family once a month. However, everything had to be written in German. Besides this, the letters' contents were limited to reporting their "supposedly good condition," because each letter was subjected to SS censorship. If an inmate was found violating the rules, they could be executed.

One member of the group suggested bribing the camp's female guards or administrative personnel to smuggle letters out, but they knew that if they were informed upon, they would be executed. A cleverer solution was needed.

The very next day, four young inmates – Krystyna, Wanda, Janina, and her sister – wrote letters to their families. When Krystyna's family received her letter, her father read it aloud and they all scrutinized the text for hints about her health, but the usual blandness seemed to prevail. Nevertheless, something about the letter struck Krystyna's brother as different.

The way the letter was written was confusing, with some of the lines being short and others long, with no obvious logic. Some sentences broke abruptly midway through, only to continue on the next line, and there were also mistakes in several of the names mentioned in the letter. He determined that his sister had deliberately placed mistakes to attract his attention and to signal the presence of a secret message embedded in the text.

His sister mentioned in it their admiration for the children's book, *Satan from the Seventh Grade,* recalling how amazed she and her brother had been at the protagonist's cleverness and resourcefulness.

He found the mention of the book odd. Why was his sister suddenly referring to a book they had adored as children? But then he remembered the novel's plot, and understood the hint.

The Czyz family worked on it until they figured out the hidden code. The girls had used urine to hide their true communication. Jeannie read on. Some twenty-seven letters written in urine by Polish women inmates reporting on the gruesome medical experiments performed on them by Nazi concentration camp doctors made it outside the camp.

Urine loses its color quickly when in contact with paper, and it becomes invisible. However, if the paper is heated, the writing reappears. These four brave and resourceful women provided first-hand statements about Nazi crimes against humanity inside the camps of Ravensbruck. With courage and daring, the small group of inmates managed to send out reports about the crimes being perpetrated in the camp. *Detwrick must have discovered their code while assigned to Ravenbruck.* Jeannie closed her computer and had a thought. She called Ismail's wife.

38

CHAPTER

LOMAX ADDRESSED JEANNIE'S teams, telling them the story of the women at the Ravensbruck concentration camp and the technique they used of concealing their communications by using urine. He dismissed them, saying that once Jeannie deciphered the rest of the diary, they would regroup.

Two hours later, Jeannie heard a knock at her front door. There was Ismail in his wheelchair with his wife. "Hey," Ismail said, "I'm here to save your ass, as always." Jeannie smiled. Her Ismail was back. After giving Jeannie a hug, his wife took off shopping, telling the two to text her when they were through.

Once she left, Jeannie pointed to her ironing board. "What's this? I thought I had to help you solve a case, not iron your undies."

"Relax, big guy. You will not be ironing my undies. Besides, if you saw my sexy underwear, you might have a relapse."

"Very funny. Okay, what do you have going on?" Jeannie gave him a rundown of Lomax's discovery. "Damn, I didn't know you could write with your own piss. And the heat from an iron can bring the letters back, huh? I got to see this."

"Okay. What do you want to do? Iron the individual pages, or take photos with my phone?"

"Well, since I am already down here if you can lower your ironing board, I can iron or take pictures, or we can switch. Whatever you want, boss lady." Jeannie wanted to give him a big hug, but then he would accuse her of getting "all Hallmark" on him, so she didn't.

"I will start with the ironing, in case I damage the evidence, then I will take the heat, pun intended," Jeannie said, testing to see if the iron was hot. "Let the games begin."

At first, it seemed like it was going to take forever because there were so many pages, but after a while, she and Ismail determined exactly how much time the heat had to be applied, and they got into a rhythm. They switched jobs several times. Ismail got upset when she asked him how he was doing. *Typical male.*

As more and more information leaped off the pages, both Ismail and Jeannie got very excited.

Detwrick, under orders from Goering, took many trips from the Mauthausen camp to the Salzkammergut mountain range so he could determine the most direct route with the least number of obstacles. The area contained the Traun River and numerous glacial lakes and raised bogs.

"Can you believe this asshole?" Ismail said while photographing and writing down the German letters that Jeannie interpreted. "He lives and eats in a death camp at night and then takes a nice drive to the mountains in the day."

"Yeah, sick bastard, huh? This is interesting. He writes here that the region has a lot of salt mines. I read or heard that the Nazis stored a lot of their stolen loot in salt mines and caves. I wonder why Goering wanted a tunnel. Why not put the stuff in a ready-made mine?"

"Maybe he did and never told Detwrick, or maybe the Nazis knew they were running out of time, and if they could hide a fully loaded train, less manpower needed," Ismail said.

"Maybe."

A few hours went by, and Ismail's wife called. "Hello, my darling," Ismail said upon answering. "No, we have several more pages to go. Yeah, that would be nice. Okay, see you soon." She's going to bring us some food from your Taco Bell. Hope that is alright. You know I have to keep my body fit in case the Chippendale's call me to add me to their revue."

"Was it the shot to your head that caused these delusions, or do they come naturally?" *Yes, Ismail was back. Thank you, Jesus.*

When Ismail's wife returned with their food, Jeannie offered to drive Ismail home once they wrapped things up. They exchanged cars since it would be easier for Ismail to get in and out of their car versus her Corvette. Plus, where in the hell would they put his wheelchair? They exchanged hugs, and after giving Ismail a kiss, his wife was on her way.

Two and a half hours later, they were finished. Jeannie felt the time fly by due to both the excitement of discovering the location of Hitler's train and their shared comradery. She grabbed two sodas, and the two of them sat at her kitchen table munching on leftover chips and salsa.

"What now?" Ismail asked. "I mean, you know where the gold train is unless the asshole lied, and this whole thing is bogus, and he's laughing at us from hell."

"I asked Lomax the same question, and he said that if the train is found, the case will be tied up in court for years to come. You know, Ace, I could not have done this without you."

"Well, you know, Sherlock had his Doctor Watson."

"Yes, and I have my Barney Fife."

"Now is the time. The woman driving off in that Corvette left Agent Loomis inside the house with the cripple. It should be easy to take them both out," Klaus Hoffman said to Jurgen Lange. Klaus was the picture boy for the SS. Standing at 6'2" with blond hair and blue eyes, Hitler would have been pleased. Not so about Jurgen, who was thirty pounds overweight and had male pattern baldness setting in, but between the two, he was the most aggressive.

They pulled down their black ski masks and checked their suppressed weapons. "Okay, let's go," Klaus said. They got out of their tan Infinite and walked towards the front door. Jurgen reached the door first and was preparing to kick it in.

"Can I help you?" Delores asked, raising her Glock 9mm. Klaus turned and fired, but the shot missed. Delores fired back and hit him in the right leg. Jurgen, in shock, did not pull his weapon but grabbed Klaus and quickly retreated with him to their car. Klaus fired one more shot at Delores but missed again. Delores fired a second shot hitting the back window of the car, shattering the glass.

Jeannie grabbed her gun from the counter after the first shot, leaving Ismail in the kitchen. She unlocked the deadbolt and looked outside before exiting the house. She saw Delores firing a second shot at a vehicle that was making a turn out of the subdivision. The rear window shattered upon impact. "Delores are you alright? What happened?" Walter came running up with his handgun at his side. "Honey, are you okay?"

"What? I can't hear you!" Delores shouted. "What?" Jeannie grabbed Delores' gun and put it in the waistband of her sweatpants. She pulled out her cell phone and dialed 9-1-1. "This is FBI agent Jeannie Loomis." While talking to the 9-1-1 operator and slowly getting information from Delores, whose hearing was starting to return, an APB was issued for two men driving a tan Infinite coup. She then called Lomax and filled him in as to what had transpired. "The Organization knows we have the diary. We have a mole," he said.

39

CHAPTER

"The FBI has Detwrick's diary. They thought it was in code, but they found that he wrote it like those filthy Jews, using his own urine."

"Yes, yes, I know that. We were unsuccessful in getting it from the FBI agent who lives in Newark. Klaus was shot, but he will recover. Do they know the location of the train?" Heiliger asked.

"They know it exists, and before they discovered he was not writing in code but in urine, they believed it was in Austria. If they know the exact location, they have not shared it. Once I learn more, I will call you."

***

Driving back after dropping off Ismail several hours later than she expected due to the shooting event, Jeannie called Lomax. "Sir, I have a lot of information, but I don't think we should discuss it over the phone. I want to call Darcy and have her make sure she, Burk, Carter, and the two Mossad agents are there early tomorrow morning if you concur. I don't think we should mention the shooting at my house. There is a chance they could hear something about it on television, but that is a chance we will have to take."

Pastries, coffee, and tea were presented to Jeannie's team as she delivered the new information she and Ismail had discovered. "First, I have to announce that you will no longer need to continue your research on the various concentration and extermination camps." Everyone started to applaud. "The tunnel is at the base of a mountain called Dachstein, which is part of the Salzkammergut range in north-central Austria. It stands at 9,826 feet above sea level. It's all there. The route, the logistics; he even included the number of Jews used during the construction of the new railroad line and tunnel."

Once the job was completed, Goering arranged for the delivery of the train and its eventual sealing in. He even sent an enormous metal gate and lock and had the key given to Detwrick. Each box car also had a heavy-duty lock. The labor force used in the completion of the track and storing of the train was shipped back to Mauthausen and gassed. There was no mention of what happened to the SS attachment used to supervise the labor force, but my guess is they, too, were eliminated."

"Now, you will love this. After the train was delivered, Detwrick secured the large gate, which was camouflaged with shrubs and rocks to blend into the mountain. Detwrick was ordered to bring the key and maps of the location to the Führerbunker. By this time, the war had definitely turned against Germany. For several days before his trip to Berlin, Detwrick helped himself to the spoils and, well, you know the rest. He made a set of keys and a copy of the map, and he kept the diary a secret. There is a lot more that I will tell you later."

"When he went to the Führerbunker, only Hitler and a few deluded Nazis believed the war was not lost. Hitler was still sending orders to units that no longer existed in the hope of pushing the Allies back. Detwrick met with Hitler, explained the location of the train using his maps, surrendered his key, and then left. Several days later, he was captured."

"The diary and his spoils were hidden in an unknown salt mine near the base of the mountain containing the train. He wrote in his diary that he waited several months after his release from Spandau prison before venturing to the mine and collecting the gold and other valuables he had hidden and then making it all the way to San Francisco. He did visit the train one additional time after his release and took gold bars and a few paintings. He talks about how he took a hit every time he cashed in a gold bar, but he still had a fortune. Apparently, he never returned to the tunnel after that."

"Excellent job. Amazing," Lomax said.

"Well, I can't take all the credit. I arranged for Ismail to help me at my house."

"I bet he loved it," Lomax said.

"Yes, he did."

Lomax cleared his throat. "Now, we have to decide what to do with all this information. If we just turn it over to Washington, we will be cut out of the loop. We will never know what happened and sadly, I would not put it past some of our corrupt political types to get their hands on it instead of those countries directly involved and deserving the spoils."

40

CHAPTER

"UNIT ONE, THE subject is approaching the apartment now. He is wearing a black jacket and baseball cap."

"Alright. Let's continue to monitor the activity inside the room before we take them down."

The five Department of Justice agents continued to monitor the conversation inside room 308. "What did you learn today?" someone asked in German. A DOJ agent quickly typed his interpretation on a screen so the other agents could read it.

"The FBI has located the Führer's train. All we were told was that it is near Linz. I wrote down the name of the mountain and as much information as I could without drawing attention to myself. Detwrick wrote the exact location in his diary using his own piss. What shall I tell Heiliger? The Organization wants the location so they can move on it, but I still don't know it."

"Mueller said that they should have taken more time and taken everything when they broke into Detwrick's house. We would already have the diary and not have wasted so much time. What good was it killing those FBI agents? We got shit; that's what we got."

"Assault time. We got an admission. Take them down."

The door to the apartment was breached so quickly that neither Mueller nor Hans could focus on a target. "Department of Justice. Put your hands in the air." Mueller got one shot off before he took two in the chest. Hans didn't get a shot off in time. Carter ran to the bathroom and slammed the door. Two agents ran to the door and began kicking it in, making sure to avoid any shots from Carter through the door.

One final kick and the door flew open. "DOJ!" one of the two agents shouted, finding Carter on the floor near the toilet with foam coming from his mouth. The smell of almonds filled the bathroom. Cyanide had taken care of this Nazi.

Lomax's phone rang. He recognized the number of his counterpart in the Department of Justice, Thomas Lynch. "Lynch, what do you have?" Lomax asked.

"You were right, but unfortunately, your Agent Carter killed himself with cyanide. Guess he wanted to go out like Goering. There were no other documents in the apartment except personal property, but we have all their cell phones and will have them analyzed. The phone that Carter was using before our forced entry shows the last listed number, but I'm sure whoever was on the other end of the line is long gone. I'll keep you in the loop."

"He was a mole from the Organization? How did you know?" Jeannie asked Lomax when he called and gave her the information.

"I guess it was just gut instinct. When you told me how energetic he was about the whole Hitler phantom train investigation and how he volunteered to work with our two Mossad agents, Darcy, and Burk, a red flag went up. Like you, I was very suspicious of Lieberman and his partner. Hell, I had suspicions about the first two Mossad agents they sent. But I guess it boiled down to Carter violating that old law enforcement adage."

"And that is?"

"Rookies should be seen, not heard. I contacted a source inside the DOJ and told him about my suspicions. He offered to put a tail on Carter. Sure enough, he led them back to an apartment that the hotel manager said was occupied by two German nationals. When the apartment was empty, the DOJ planted a few bugs, and they started monitoring.

I had hoped that at least one of them would've survived so we could learn more about the Organization, but their SS oath to the death really meant something to them. Goldman told me before that he even suspects possible Organization individuals in his own department, and that got me thinking."

"Well, if that was their only source, I wonder what they will do now trying to locate the train?"

"I thought about that too, after I learned of the shooting. What did Carter learn from his time with your team? Assuming the last call he was going to make was to relay what he learned at the briefing, then the Organization only knows it is somewhere in Austria in that mountain that I cannot pronounce, so we should be okay."

"I have a request, sir. We lost three good people in the Grand Street house, plus Ismail almost died and may end up crippled, though I hope not."

"You forgot to add that you and our Mossad friends also got shot," Lomax added.

"Well, there's that too. Sir, I would like permission to fly to our agency in Austria and supervise the discovery of the ghost train."

***

"Mr. Goldman, Lomax here. I'm really sticking my neck out and could be fired for what I am about to tell you, but in the spirit of being Allies......"

41

CHAPTER

Most Americans are unaware that the FBI operates outside of its borders. There are 63 legal attaché offices—commonly known as legats—and 30 smaller suboffices in key cities around the globe, providing coverage for more than 180 countries, territories, and islands. Each office is established through mutual agreement with the host country and is situated in the US embassy or consulate in that nation. One such office is in Vienna.

The flight alone from San Francisco to Vienna took almost fourteen hours. Add to that an additional two hours and thirty-minute layover in Amsterdam, and Jeannie had over a sixteen-hour trip ahead of her. *Can't believe that, once again, I am entering Austria, who, only a few years ago, wanted me to be extradited to face a bogus charge of murder.*

Jeannie still had some Vicodin she had not taken while rehabbing after being shot. She took two pills that she knew would put her asleep, and told the flight attendant not to wake her for meals. Upon arrival, she took the city airport train to the city center in Vienna, which was near the American Embassy.

She checked into the Harmonie Vienna Hotel and instantly fell asleep after a hot shower and a light room service meal. When she woke and got her bearings, she pulled one of the last entries from her purse pertaining to the day the phantom gold train arrived and was turned over to Detwrick.

Today, our Führer's gold train was transferred to me. The train is magnificent. One of only a few specially built high-speed machines. Its armor plating could withstand anything except a direct bomb attack from above. The train contains twenty-one box cars. One of those is a coach car for the SS attachment. Each car has a large swastika as well as a formidable lock.

When the train arrived, the engine had our flag draped over its nose and two SS soldiers mounted to either side of every other car, plus a few standing on top of the train. On the roof of the last boxcar lay a massive iron door. This was my proudest moment. Adolf Hitler, my Führer, had entrusted me with the future of the Fourth Reich.

The SS detachment was transferred over to my supervision. I am sure they knew the contents of the boxcars, but they, like the Jews, who probably had similar knowledge, will not be able to use it after I secure the train in the mountain. That would also include the train conductor and other train personnel.

I climbed into the locomotive and ordered the conductor to proceed at a slow speed until I told him to stop. The train continued down the track. Once we entered a heavily forested area, I told him to stop. On the side of the track were several other SS guards and a few Jewish workers standing by a large crane. I motioned to the Jews to hook the chain from the crane to the metal door on the roof of the last car and raise it. Once they had, I instructed the conductor to reverse slightly so the metal door could be secured to the front of the locomotive after I removed our flag.

Once secured, I walked further down the track and on the right side, found the switch that would take the train off its current path and divert it into the mountain range. Once back on the locomotive, we continued, but at an even more reduced speed. We heard machinegun fire which told me that the SS had eliminated the Jews near the crane.

We moved on. The conductor asked me how much further. I did not have to answer him since, as we made a slight right-hand turn, he saw that the track was beginning to enter a slight incline. I ordered the conductor to sound his whistle several times. It was quite beautiful climbing the mountain with my Führer's treasure.

After another half an hour or so, I saw SS guards standing on the side of the track with more Jews, awaiting our arrival. I told the conductor that we had finally reached our destination and that he must stop exactly when I told him so that the gate could be removed and installed, after which the train could be driven into the tunnel. That was his final entry about the train and its whereabouts.

The next morning, she arrived at the FBI station in Vienna. "Agent Loomis, I hope you had a nice uneventful trip," SAC Keith Henderson asked while shaking her hand. Henderson was probably in his early fifties, by Jeannie's guess. With blond hair and striking blue eyes, he stood about six inches above Jeannie. He was wearing a tan-colored long-sleeved sweater and black slacks. *Very handsome man.*

"Long, but yes, uneventful. I could sure go for some American coffee, though."

"Right this way." After getting her coffee, Henderson led her to a small conference room where five other agents were sitting. "Ladies and gentlemen, let me introduce ASSC Loomis from our San Francisco bureau."

"Please, call me Jeannie. With a cup of American coffee in hand, she walked around and shook everyone's hand, then she walked towards a table with a map. "I see you have a map ready, so let's get started." She didn't get far, as everyone wanted to know more details about Detwrick and the whole evolution of Hitler's gold train mystery. Jeannie gave them the shortest synopsis she could. After bringing the Austrian FBI staff up to speed, Jeannie opened her briefcase and pulled out portions of Detwrick's diary.

Using the details, she laid out a possible route to the phantom train.

Agent Susan Connelly, an avid hiker and in great shape, suggested a way to approach the mountain from a different route that might save some time. Jeannie later learned that Connelly had only been with the FBI in Washington for three years before being transferred to Austria. *That is very unusual. I wonder how she managed that?*

"Hey, you know the area, I don't," Jeannie said. "Whatever works." Turning to Henderson. "Did my SAC explain that we will be joined by two Mossad agents?"

"Yes, he did. Can we trust them?" he asked.

"They could have jeopardized our investigation many times but instead offered valuable information, so yes, we can trust them."

"That's good enough for me. When will they get here?"

"I expect them sometime today, for sure, by the time we set out tomorrow morning."

"Also," she looked at the assembled group, "If we manage to find the ghost train, we will have to arrange for it to be guarded until the various governments can figure out what to do with the fortune it contains."

"I already have that in motion. If we are successful, the Austrian government, as well as neutral countries, will send soldiers to secure it. God, can you envision the hearings that will take place to see who will get all that loot?" Henderson said.

42

CHAPTER

JEANNIE, JOSEPH ALDERMAN, Eleazar Lieberman, and five members of the Austrian FBI team set out for the site of the Mauthausen memorial. It was a day trip from Vienna to the concentration camp. Taking two cars, the five agents, Jeannie, and the two Mossad agents arrived at their lodging, the Donauhof Hotel, 1.2 miles from the camp. The hotel had two restaurants and a very nice bar. Jeannie would share a room with Agent Sarah Richards, an eight-year veteran agent.

By leaving Vienna at daybreak, their arrival at Mauthausen allowed Jeannie and several of the agents to take the last tour of the infamous camp. Alderman and Lieberman remained behind. They did not need a reminder of the brutality of their countrymen that took place here.

Jeannie felt it was ironic since they took a train from the hotel for 1.2 miles to reach the camp. She was sure that Detwrick had used this same railway line numerous times. She also felt weird when they arrived, seeing a bistro on the ground in the camp. She could understand the need to preserve the site as a memorial so people would not forget what happened here, but a restaurant?

The tour began with the guide giving everyone an admonition:

"The Mauthausen concentration camp was a site of the suffering and death of thousands of people during the Nazi dictatorship. To preserve the dignity of the site and to enhance public safety, visitor regulations are in place for all visitors and apply to all areas of the memorial site. By entering the memorial complex, you agree to abide by these regulations. We do not advise visiting the Mauthausen Memorial with children under the age of 14.

As soon as the tour guide started to discuss the atrocities by the SS against the Jewish prisoners, she noticed a change in Sarah's behavior.

"Are you okay? No offense, but you don't look too good," Jeannie said.

"I think I will be fine." She paused. "I am Jewish. Both of my great grandparents on my father's side died in Auschwitz. I have heard all the stories of their horrible life living under the Nazis until they were transported to their death. I need to see this. I must someday tell my children about life in the camps.

"Do you have children?" Jeannie asked.

"No, I am not married. Right now, I want to focus on my career with the bureau. Maybe that sounds strange. Someday, I will have a husband and children. Are you married, and do you have children?"

"No, I am not married and have no kids." She decided not to reveal the loss of her unborn in a shootout while stationed in Roseville, California. "I've been married twice, and for what it is worth, I think you are making the right decision on holding off for now. I love my job, but the travel and stress caused my two divorces. At least, that's what I tell myself."

The guide, using a small megaphone, started her memorized speech. "*From 1938 to 1945, the Mauthausen concentration camp was at the center of a system of over 40 subcamps and was the main site of political, social, and racist persecution by the National Socialist regime on Austrian territory. Of a total of around 190,000 people imprisoned here, at least 90,000 were murdered.*

An hour and a half later, the tour ended. Throughout the whole tour, Jeannie looked at the various buildings and wondered where Detwrick might have stood, eaten, and slept. *Ninety thousand innocent people slaughtered, yet that bastard lived until he was 101 years old. Maybe someday, if she made it to heaven, God could explain why.*

The eight of them had drinks and dinner together. Most of their discussion had to do with their careers with the FBI and how they ended up in beautiful Austria. A few knew of the cases Jeannie was involved in and wanted to learn the particulars. Others wanted to know about the two Mossad agents and about Israel. A few bitched about the bullshit coming from the administration in D.C. It wasn't until after dinner that they began discussing the train and how they hoped to find it. Agent Connelly pulled out a map she had showing the terrain. She also pulled out her iPad and turned it on.

Jeannie was really impressed with her background. Both her father and brother were professional mountain climbing guides, so naturally, Connelly followed in their footsteps until she joined the FBI. Now, hiking in the mountains was just her way of staying in shape.

"I think, if we start here and proceed in this direction, we can cover the most ground. If we start early again, we should have enough time to get there and back down the mountain before nighttime. Just in case, I brought some hiking gear and some food for the trip up and back. I sent a drone up there late yesterday afternoon. This is what we are up against." She turned the monitor around so everyone could see the drone flyover. *God, I wish I hadn't stopped going to the gym. This climb might just kill me.*

The morning looked clear when they set out, although it was chilly from a breeze coming down from the mountain. They drove as close to the base of the mountain as they could and then set off on foot. The characteristics of the mountain changed from the base to the summit. First, a deciduous forest made up of oak, beech, and fir trees gave way higher up to larch and pine. Deer, rabbits, and a few pheasants fled as the group encroached on their territory. A heavy dew clung to the trees and ferns, brushing off on them as they made their ascent.

There was no sign of a railroad track, but according to Detwrick's diary, he had the Jews dismantle the track after the train was secured and burn the wooden support structure after removing the rails. Jeannie realized that seventy-seven years had passed since the end of the war, and nature had done a pretty good job of reclaiming the area. Fortunately, some of the physical landmarks Detwrick mentioned could still be found. He mentioned that the main landscape pointing to the tunnel was Hitler's Cliff, whatever the hell that meant.

"Okay. Let's see if we can visualize this place during World War II. Detwrick had his forced labor construct a train trestle and a ramp up to the place where the tunnel was being made. So, if we each look at the mountain from different positions, maybe we can come up with a consensus from here up to somewhere up there," Jeannie said, shading her eyes as she looked up to the summit. She realized while pointing that the area was huge. In doing so, she remembered Lomax's history lesson about the Romans having to build a ramp to reach the fortress, Masada, on a mountain top.

She thought about how ridiculous they must look, walking around the area together, looking at the same mountain. Everyone shared their thoughts about where Detwrick might have started his ramp. "I don't think it would have been too high up. Remember, Detwrick was on a tight time schedule. The ramp and tunnel had to be finished, and the pressure increased when he was told the train was on its way," Jeannie offered.

"Therefore, the ramp probably didn't have to go higher than maybe the midpoint," she added. Everyone agreed on a position on the mountain where it appeared the terrain was right for a ramp, but the heavy forest made it hard to view the contour of the mountain at the higher elevations from their current position.

"This is not going to be easy," Agent Connelly said. "It looks like there have been several landslides over the years, and the entrance to the tunnel, if there is one, may be sealed forever."

The thought had also crossed Jeannie's mind.

"I think the best thing we can do is encircle the base from that position (pointing to a location on the mountain). If anyone finds something interesting, shout it out on the radio, and we will meet you. Even though the climb back down the mountain will be easier, we must hurry."

Jeannie began heading east, keeping Sarah in sight on her right and Henderson on her left. The last thing she wanted to happen was to get lost on the damn mountain. Lieberman and Alderman were several yards away. Some areas required Jeannie to turn back and take another route due to rough terrain or heavy foliage. Time passed, and no one found anything.

At noon, Connolly was on the radio advising everyone to take a short lunch break. *Thank God.* Jeannie dug into her backpack and pulled at one of the sandwiches Connelly had got for everyone. Jeannie's leg muscles ached. *Need to get back to the gym, that's for damn sure.*

Fifteen minutes later, Connolly announced it was time to continue the search.

Jeannie was getting frustrated. Tired, sore, and upset over her physical condition, she felt that if there was a train, it was lost to time and the elements.

Twenty minutes passed. The radio crackled. "Hey, everyone. Over here," Connelly said. "I think I found something."

43

CHAPTER

SLIPPING AND SLIDING, with cuts on both her hands, Jeannie was the third person to reach Connelly. The craggy terrain fought their access all the way up the incline. At first, all she saw was a pile of small rocks, but they didn't blend into the other rocks and boulders of the mountain. Then she realized it was building material brought in by the Jewish slaves to lay the rails for the train. The wooden ties were long gone, ordered burned by Detwrick.

Connolly pointed to a position where a ledge extended out of the mountain. "Does that look like a fucking Hitler salute to anyone?" There, a section of the mountain displayed an outcropping that did look like the common Nazi salute.

Jeannie's heart was racing in excitement, or was it the climb over from her previous position? *This has to be the site.* "Looks like it to me. You did good, girl." Jeannie said while trying to catch her breath.

Henderson attempted to climb a large pile of rocks up towards the ledge but kept sliding down. Connolly, the hiking expert, decided to give it a try but first pulled out a climbing rope from her backpack. "If I can make it up there, I will secure the rope and throw it down to you." *You go, gal. I need a Subway sandwich and diet Dr. Pepper,* Jeannie thought.

Connolly made it look easy. After only a few slides, she made it to the side of the outcropping and excitedly said that she had found what looked like a large metal door. She threw down the rope.

Henderson motioned for Jeannie to go first. Even without gloves, the rope did not burn her hands, although the small cuts from her previous falls objected. Out of breath, she reached Connolly, who offered her hand for her final ascent. While waiting for the other members to make the climb, Jeannie and Connolly cut away some foliage with the folded saw Connelly had brought.

By the time everyone made it up the pile of rocks, enough material had been removed to reveal a massive metal wall with huge hinges and a custom-made padlock. The gate was very high, high enough for a train locomotive to enter. "Looks like it's approximately 20' tall and what, 15 or more feet wide," Jeannie said.

"That sounds about right for the height and width of locomotives in the 1940s," Henderson said. He noticed several people looking at him. "Hey, what can

I say? I like trains and have a lot of books about trains used through the ages."

"I'd say you are pretty close in your estimates, Jeannie. You could put a big-ass train inside there, that's for sure. If this is the tunnel, how far back do you think it goes?" Henderson asked.

"Detwrick said it had twenty boxcars, not counting the coach car used by the SS security team and the engine, so fairly large. The bigger question is, how are we going to open this damn door?" Jeannie pounded on the door just to see how solid it was and was amazed when a rusted section fell to the ground. The sound echoed around the mountain. She looked at Connolly. "Oh please, make it that easy." It would not be.

Connolly tried unsuccessfully to move the padlock; it was fixed solidly to the gate itself, encrusted with rust and moss. "Since no one knows what happened to the key after Detwrick gave it to Hitler unless we can somehow break the lock, we will need to focus on the damn door." Everyone agreed.

"Too bad old Detwrick did not leave a duplicate of the key in his safe," Henderson said.

"Nothing in this case has come easily," Jeannie replied.

Assessing the size and weight of the large door, the eight realized that, at a minimum, a sledgehammer and pick would be required to break away part of the door to gain entrance. They would have to return tomorrow with the proper tools. They grabbed the foliage they had removed and placed it back to conceal the gate. The secret inside the tunnel would have to wait until their return tomorrow

***

"Yes, we have found the tunnel. Yes, we will see the actual train when we go back up tomorrow with more equipment and open the entrance. Once we can get inside the tunnel, I will examine the train. Our Führer's dream of financing a Fourth Reich will soon be a reality. How will you know when to send in the assault team? I cannot set off a flare."

***

Jeannie really enjoyed Sarah's company. When not thinking about the death camp a little over a mile away from their hotel, she laughed and joked both with Jeannie and the other agents over drinks and dinner that night. Jeannie was thinking of asking her if she might consider a transfer to her San Francisco office. Maybe later.

Sarah used to live in Hawaii, where she gave surfing lessons. As great as it was, she realized it was not a career and continued her studies at the University of Hawaii. She graduated with a degree in sociology and decided on a career with the FBI. She ranked third in her class at Quantico and was fascinated by behavioral profiling. She remembered Jeannie's name in a few of her lectures from the time Jeannie taught there.

She was currently taking online courses to earn her master's degree in psychology and hoped that, after earning her degree, she might be accepted to the behavioral analysis unit.

All but Henderson decided to call it a night. He remained at the bar. Bright and early the next morning, back up the mountain they'd go.

Jeannie called Lomax and gave him an update. He'd told her to call no matter what time it was. "Sure sounds like you found Hitler's gold train," he said

"Oh, it's there. I just feel it. I will send you some photos when I hang up showing the metal gate we found today. I just hope we can remove enough of the door to get inside. One of the female agents went to a store when we returned and got more equipment for the task. You should see the size of the gate and the padlock Goering had Detwrick use. It was ingenious how Detwrick transferred the gigantic door off the train and up the mountain. I will take more pictures, including what we find inside the box cars, and send them to you tomorrow. Now, it's time to get some well-earned sleep."

"The climb up the mountain went quicker the next morning since they knew their destination. A thick fog shrouded the mountain, and there was a constant drizzle. Those wearing hats had water droplets falling off their beaks, including Jeannie. Halfway up, they took a short break. Everyone was eager to arrive at the tunnel entrance, but Connolly said they had to pace themselves so no one would get injured.

Finally, they made it. Everyone stood back as Henderson took the first whacks at the door. Each time the sledgehammer hit the gate, another echo vibrated through the mountain range. The other two male agents, as well as Alderman and Lieberman, took their turns assaulting the gate. More and more rust fell from the façade, but it stood firm. "Probably should have brought an acetylene torch with us," Connolly said. "Or maybe dynamite," she said, laughing. Everyone joined in and agreed.

"I suggest concentrating on the area adjacent to the hinges. They seem to have taken the brunt of the weather over the years," she added. At first, it did not seem to be any more productive than the other areas of the giant gate.

Finally, after another swing of the hammer, a new sound came from the gate, more of a hollow sound. Everyone looked at each other, seeing if they had all heard the change in the pitch from the strike. A follow-up swing created the same sound. They had found a weak spot. Each of the males increased the frequency of their swings. A six-inch section near the middle hinge broke and fell as pebbles to the ground. Jeannie walked forward and asked to look inside. There was just enough space to allow her to stare inside while using her flashlight. Everyone waited to hear her report. "Ladies and gentlemen, there is a big-ass train inside this tunnel." Everyone cheered.

The gate reluctantly began falling apart. A section approximately one foot by two feet, when bent back and forth, came loose. Connolly grabbed a flashlight and put her head and flashlight further inside than Jeannie had managed. She did not react. She pulled her head back out and turned off the flashlight. "Yep! Hitler's train is inside. It is no longer a phantom train."

Everyone took turns squeezing into the small opening and looking into the tunnel. There was an odor emanating from the cave, like when Jeannie visited the Mammoth Cave in Kentucky. Water could be seen on the sides of the train dripping from the ceiling.

Jeannie grabbed her phone and began taking pictures of the entrance to the tunnel and a few after putting her hand back into the ever-larger gate opening. *Probably one of the greatest historical finds of this century,* she thought.

44

CHAPTER

EVEN AFTER YEARS of concealment, the solid metal door continued to resist the assault by the agents slamming the sledgehammer and pick against it. Finally, another larger section fell away. A few more feet and there would be a safe entrance through the gate for the group to enter the interior of the tunnel.

"BANG" echoed through the mountain range as the final section broke away from the gate and fell to the ground. It was as if the gate said, "you win."

Everyone looked at Jeannie, non-verbally inviting her to be the first to enter. Flashlight in hand, in she went. The last car of the train came into view about fifty feet inside. It looked huge, with only five feet of clearance from the walls on both sides. *Thank God I am not claustrophobic.* She could hear the rest of the team enter the opening as she continued further in. Using the flashlight, she counted twenty-one cars and the engine. Sounds of everyone's footsteps filled the cavernous structure as their feet splashed in the moisture on the ground.

Examining the first boxcar she came to, she saw a huge swastika on the side plus a large padlock, alike but smaller than the one on the entrance gate. Henderson hit the lock with a pick. After two strikes, it broke. The moment of truth had arrived.

Attention again fell on Jeannie, urging her to open the cattle car. She removed the remnants of the lock and tried to open it, but the combination of rust and the weight of the door prevented her. Three men, working together, finally got the door to budge, but they then turned the remaining task back over to Jeannie.

After pushing hard, the door began to slide. Susan and Sarah illuminated the inside with their flashlights. "Oh, my God," Sarah gasped. The entire car gave up its shrouded mystery after over seventy-seven years. A bright yellow cast was shining from stacks and stacks of gold bars, only partially concealed by tarp material, most of which had rotted away over time.

The group moved on to the next car. The lock was removed in a similar fashion, and the door was pushed out. This boxcar contained wooden boxes with more black swastikas painted on their sides, stacked from floor to ceiling. The boxes had been nailed shut. Again using his pick, Henderson smashed the side of one of the containers. Out poured gold fillings from human teeth. Sarah, after realizing what she was looking at, ran from the group and vomited into the water on the ground near the wall of the tunnel.

Jeannie pulled a tissue from her purse and handed it to Sarah. Alderman and Lieberman just stared at the boxes filled with fillings. Jeannie couldn't imagine what they were thinking. The group, minus Sarah, moved on to the next car. This contained more gold bars. The next contained paintings and more boxes with the black swastika marking. This time, no attempt was made to see what was inside. All told, they investigated four boxcars, leaving the rest undisturbed.

Except for the coach car used by the SS guards, and the engine, everyone agreed it was probably more of the same. When they finished, no one spoke. Jeannie took several photos of their finds so she could share them with Lomax and her team.

"Well, Jeannie. You solved not only a double homicide but also the mystery of the mythical phantom train. You personally stopped the Nazis from finding this gold train and using its treasure to finance their new Fourth Reich. My relatives in heaven, killed by these bastards, thank you," Sarah said. Several agents clapped their hands.

"I guess now is the time for you to call in security from the various countries and secure the site, Jeannie said to Henderson while still embracing Sarah.

"Yes, I'll do it now while I get a smoke." He pulled his satellite phone out of his pocket along with a pack of cigarettes and began walking back towards the entrance of the tunnel.

"How many countries do you think will lay claim to the gold?" Connelly asked Jeannie.

"From what I understand from my SAC, there will be claims by Israel, Austria, Russia, and even Germany."

"Germany," Sarah said, pulling away from Jeannie. "What claim do they have? This property belongs to the Jewish community, not Germany." Alderman and Lieberman naturally agreed.

"I asked the same question of my SAC, and he said that Germany will make their claim based on the fact that the train came from their country and belongs to them," Jeannie replied.

"So, because it's their train, they still think they are entitled to the wealth it contains?" Sarah asked. Jeannie just shrugged her shoulders in reply. "Well, fuck them," Sarah added.

A few minutes later, Henderson returned to the tunnel. "I was able to get through. The first group will arrive by helicopter, and once they arrive, we will turn the site over to them and use their copters to get us down from here.

"Great," Connelly said. At least we don't have to slip and slide our way down." Everyone laughed.

Jeannie felt that something was off but could not put her finger on it. Even after their huge relief at finding the train, it did not solve the problem of how to eventually unload the train's cargo. *I guess they could run helicopter after helicopter. What a task, but it is not my concern anymore. More than likely, they will just post guards and fight among themselves on what to do next. By then, I will be home in bed and sleeping for a week.*

The group took over the empty coach car previously used by the SS guard contingent, not knowing how long they would have to wait. The car was in surprisingly good shape and comfortable. "How much do you think the valuables in these cars are worth?" Connelly asked, breaking the silence.

"If I said millions, it would be an underestimation of its value," Henderson said. "I bet we are talking billions and billions of dollars, and that doesn't include those rare paintings we saw."

"In our country, we have many binders containing lists of the proper owners of many of the paintings stolen over time by the Nazis. I am sure that list will be compared with the paintings in these cars in the hopes of reuniting them with their owners or their relatives," Alderman said.

"But what about all those gold and silver teeth fillings? How does one go about deciding who gets that money?" Sarah asked. No one answered, knowing how the fillings were gathered in the death camps.

Over an hour passed, and several complained of getting hungry before the unmistakable sound of an approaching helicopter filled the interior of the tunnel. "It's time," Henderson said as the group climbed out of the SS car. They began walking towards the entrance of the tunnel and saw several individuals dressed in black rappel from the copter. "How are we supposed to get up there? Can't they get closer?" Sarah asked. No one answered.

The first two figures from the helicopter reached the entrance to the tunnel and looked at the group. The two men snapped to attention giving the Hitler salute when they saw Henderson, who was at the back.

Everyone started to laugh except Henderson. The men looked at him. He pulled out his weapon and trained it on the group. "Don't worry, Sarah, you and the others won't have to go back down the mountain or be pulled up to a helicopter. Now, everyone, please place your weapons on the ground."

"Well played, Henderson. Another damn modern-day Nazi. How long have you been a member of the Organization?" Jeannie asked.

"For generations, Jeannie, going back to my great-grandfather, who was a proud member of the Waffen SS. Now, I will ask you one more time to drop your weapons on the ground."

He gave orders in German to the two men, which Jeannie knew were instructions to escort them back to the SS car. In the distance, a second copter could be heard approaching. "You and the Organization really believe you can resurrect the Third Reich?" Jeannie asked before one of the two men pushed Jeannie in the back.

"You have to admit, Jeannie, what you saw in our Führer's train will go a long way to financing its establishment, don't you think?"

Jeannie looked at both the Mossad agents. All three were looking for an opening to retaliate.

"How long have you been a mole in the FBI?" Sarah asked.

"I was a member of the Organization from birth. I did the same as the rest of you, well, except you two," looking at Alderman and Lieberman while waving his gun. "FBI training in Quantico, numerous transfers to various bureaus. I was just fortunate to be at the right place at the right time after you decoded Lt. Detwrick's diary."

The sound of more footsteps entering the tunnel caused Henderson to again instruct the first two men to get everyone back on the train. "Our second team is nearly here. Get them to the car and kill them," he ordered in German.

Gunfire erupted out of nowhere. Henderson was struck several times by automatic fire and fell to the wet ground. The other two turned their attention from Jeannie and the other agents and began returning gunfire towards the entrance to the tunnel. Jeannie yelled for everyone to get down.

The gunfire sound was amplified by the walls of the tunnel, and ricochets could be heard careening off the walls. One of the ricochets hit Jeannie on her left upper arm. *Not the same arm. Give me a break.* The gunfire seemed to last for a long time, but it was only a few seconds, followed by silence. Gunsmoke filled the tunnel overcoming the musty odor of the cavern.

Four people began walking toward the group. "Agent Loomis," a person shouted as the group of four men reached their location. Jeannie rose from the ground holding her arm, followed by the other agents. Henderson and his two SS comrades were lying dead on the floor.

"I'm Agent Loomis," she said, trying to focus on the men but only having the light from the opened end of the tunnel to assist her. Sarah noticed her bleeding and came over to help.

"Mossad, Agent Goldman," the person said, offering his hand. Is everyone alright?" He looked at Jeannie and saw blood on her blouse. "How bad," he asked.

"Just a scratch."

45

CHAPTER

AS ONE OF the Mossad agents from the helicopter wrapped Jeannie's arm, she learned from Goldman that Mossad had been tipped off that the Organization was watching her and his Mossad agents' progress regarding the location of the phantom train. Eight members had been surveilled for the past few days as they watched and learned of your progress, receiving intel from Henderson.

"How did you know Henderson was a mole for the Organization?" Jeannie asked.

Goldman paused before answering. "Your SAC, Lomax, asked me to do him a favor and conduct a background check on each of the five agents you would be working with for your own safety. We have a list of many of their agents, but Henderson was not there. However, we decided to observe his actions anyway. The night before you climbed back up the mountain, he left the bar of the hotel you were staying at and met with members of the Organization."

"We did not have enough men here to take them out at the time. Our earliest and best time to rescue you and the other agents was now. Fortunately, no one got seriously hurt. The other members of the Organization are in custody down below. We took over their helicopters, and here we are. So, this is the infamous phantom gold train. Looks like Hitler loses again."

"What will happen now?" Jeannie asked.

"Within the hour, Austrian, German, and French soldiers will arrive and secure the tunnel. I understand that the US has also been asked by the United Nations to provide troops. Something about claims from descendants of Jews living in America. After that, who knows how long they are going to take to unravel the redistribution of the Nazis' stolen wealth. We must assume that the Organization will try to infiltrate those assigned to guard the train so everyone will suspect each other. Well, everyone. I think it is time to get you down the mountain."

***

Two weeks later, Heiliger still felt the sting of defeat. He walked into his massive office, which had a similar SS flag to the one hanging in the main auditorium. He was wearing a dark blue designer suit and red tie, what the Americans call a power tie. Soon, he would be meeting with the second and third most powerful officers in the Organization before addressing the main body concerning the loss of Hitler's gold train.

He had already rehearsed what he would tell the gathering, that yes, it was sad to lose out on seizing the train, but he could reassure them that the Führer had many other trains, caves, tunnels, and mines containing treasure hidden away waiting to be discovered. He hoped the spin would satisfy them for a while.

He opened his humidor and pulled out a Fuente Opus X cigar that cost $100. Smoking this particular cigar when the other two powerful members entered should impress them, he thought. After using his Germanus cigar cutter, he found his jet flame lighter and rolled the cigar, getting a good light.

As he was doing so, still formulating what he would cover during his upcoming meeting, his attention was diverted to a red dot on his chest. He started to look for the source, at which point he heard the soft breaking of glass and felt a tremendous pain in his chest. His shirt turned red with blood as he fell into his desk chair. His head fell forward, hitting his desk, but he was already gone.

Ariel began to unscrew the sniper rifle while Levi put his binoculars in his backpack. With the sniper rifle packed away in its carrying case, the two turned and left the roof of the opposite building. "Another dead Nazi," Ariel said.

***

Jeannie checked in with Lomax after her home visit with Ismail. "How's he doing?"

"He's itching to get back to work, and his wife can't wait! I relayed your orders that until he gets medical clearance, no work. His leg is getting better, thank God. He is walking further and further each day without a cane. You were right; he's a fighter. Any more news about the phantom gold train?"

"They are still in the long process of trying to locate victims whose identities can be linked directly to paintings, jewelry, and so on. Various museums have also put in claims. The governments of Israel, Austria, Poland, Russia, Germany, the US, and God knows who else will be battling for ownership of the treasure on the train for years, I suspect."

"I think you will find this interesting. Heiliger, the leader of the Organization, was killed by a sniper in his office yesterday morning, or was it the day before? I can't keep up with the time difference. Anyway, he was shot in the chest by a sniper on a roof across the street. He never knew what hit him."

"Really? Any idea who the sniper was?"

"No, but I am sure the list of suspects is long. Maybe it was someone in the Organization who was pissed off at being able to seize the train for the Nazis. Hell, it might be some Nazi bastard just wanting to move up in their sadistic club. I don't think our government had anything to do with it, but I would not rule out Mossad. Unfortunately, as you know, we get rid of one asshole, and they are quickly replaced by another. Go home and get some rest. I will see you next week. That was one hell of a job you did."

46

CHAPTER

JEANNIE WAS GREETED with a nice warm Saturday morning when she woke up. The wound from the stray bullet that had grazed her arm continued to itch, but it appeared to be healing well. *Damn, girl. Shot twice in the same year. Ismail and I will no doubt compete for bragging rights.*

Laying on her kitchen counter was a book she had picked up at Barnes and Noble the night before, titled *Ravensbruck: Life and Death in Hitler's Concentration Camp for Women*.

Between looking at her koi swimming to the surface of their tank for food and preparing her breakfast, she wondered if any of the four concentration camp women who ingeniously came up with the idea of concealing hidden messages in their letters home using urine were still alive. *If not, dear God, let them know in heaven how their ingenuity stopped modern-day Nazis from seizing the phantom train.*

After breakfast, she went to a local nursery and bought two flats of inpatients, a few gardenias, azaleas, and three camelias, plus some planter mix. It pretty much maxed out the small trunk area and passenger seat of her Corvette. It was time to do some gardening in her backyard.

Once home, she placed the plants in the various areas near her community fence where she felt they would look best and got ready to start her project. "Hi, Jeannie. What a fantastic day, huh?" Delores asked, straining to see over the fence. Jeannie instantly thought of Wilson from Home Improvement again.

"Hi, Delores. Yes, it is going to be a very nice day. We might have an early summer. How are you and Walter doing?"

"Oh, we are both fine. I was wondering if you have a few minutes and could talk to Galina? She's that Russian lady who lives way down on the corner. Apparently, something has happened to her niece, and she is really broken up about it. She thinks she might have been kidnapped in Eastern Europe. I think she would feel better after talking with you.

So much for a nice leisurely day gardening in the backyard.

Epilogue

Effects of Nazi looting today

Approximately 20% of the art in Europe was looted (Raubkunst) by the Nazis, and well over 100,000 items have not been returned to their rightful owners. Most of what is still missing includes everyday objects like china, crystal, and silver. The Nazi art confiscation program has been called the greatest displacement of art in human history.

The United States Government has estimated that German forces and other Nazi agents, before and during World War II, seized or coerced the sale of one-fifth of all Western art in existence at the time; approximately a quarter of a million pieces of art. Because of such a wide displacement of Nazi-looted art from all over Europe, to this day, some tens of thousands of artworks stolen by the Nazis have not been located.

Some objects of great cultural significance remain missing, though how much has yet to be determined. This is a major issue for the art market since legitimate organizations do not want to deal in objects with unclear ownership titles.

Since the mid-1990s, after several books, magazines, and newspapers began exposing the subject to the public, many dealers, auction houses, and museums have grown more careful about checking the provenance of objects that are available for purchase in case they are looted. Some museums in the United States and elsewhere have agreed to check the provenance of works in their collections.

Coming in December:

Rollercoaster

Iraqi terrorists home in on soft targets in the United States – especially amusement parks. As the body count mounts, FBI agent Jeannie Loomis and her team race against time to stop the mayhem.

www.ingramcontent.com/pod-product-compliance
Lightning Source LLC
Chambersburg PA
CBHW060550310726
48982CB00008B/1077/J

* 9 7 8 1 7 3 7 8 7 3 6 5 5 *